THE SEVEN STONES

Terry, the Torus and the Tumblestones

BOOK ONE

THE SEVEN STONES

C. P. Goy

www.terry-torus-tumblestones.co.uk

Matador
9 De Montfort Mews
Leicester LE1 7FW, UK
Tel: (+44) 116 255 9311 / 9312
Email: books@troubador.co.uk
Web: www.troubador.co.uk/matador

ISBN 978 1848761-568

A Cataloguing-in-Publication (CIP) catalogue record for this book is
available from the British Library.

Typeset in 11.5pt Sabon by Troubador Publishing Ltd, Leicester, UK
Printed in the UK by TJ International, Padstow, Cornwall

Matador is an imprint of Troubador Publishing Ltd

For all the young readers (and those not so young) who understand that a good book can be a best friend.

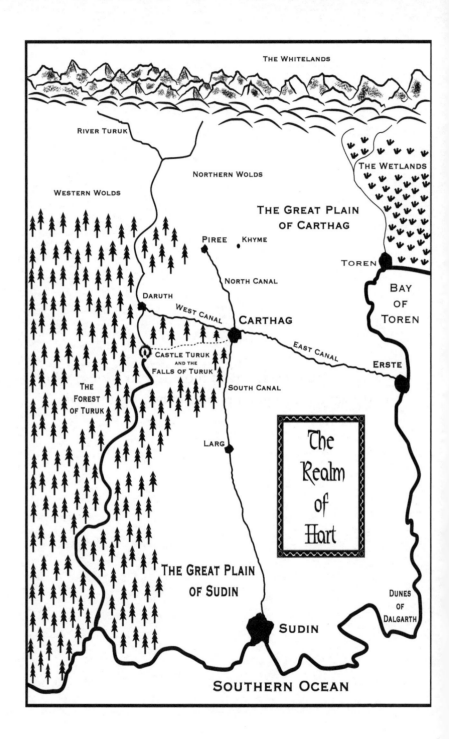

THE WHITELANDS

RIVER TURUK

THE WETLANDS

NORTHERN WOLDS

WESTERN WOLDS

THE GREAT PLAIN
OF CARTHAG

PIREE   KHYME

TOREN

NORTH CANAL

BAY
OF
TOREN

DARUTH

WEST CANAL   CARTHAG

EAST CANAL

ERSTE

CASTLE TURUK
AND THE
FALLS OF TURUK

SOUTH CANAL

THE
FOREST
OF TURUK

LARG

The
Realm
of
Hart

THE GREAT PLAIN
OF SUDIN

DUNES
OF
DALGARTH

SUDIN

SOUTHERN OCEAN

Contents

Crow Wood

Terry was thinking four different thoughts at once. If these thoughts could have been untangled, and put into a sensible order, they would have run something like this:

I'm in the ruin of Huntsman's Cottage, in the middle of Crow Wood.
I'm by myself.
It's nearly dark.
Something very strange is happening.

Nobody had lived in the Huntsman's Cottage for a long, long time. Ivy had crept up all of the outside walls, smothering even the upstairs windows. It couldn't climb any higher than the eaves, but as if to continue the theme, a small tree had managed to take root in one of the chimneys. When it came to the roof, things were no better. On the north side, a carpet of purple-green moss hid whatever lay beneath, and on the south side, it looked as if a giant fist had punched it. This was only because some of the rafters underneath had rotted and collapsed, but still, the effect was impressive. To make matters even worse, a few of the grey slate tiles had taken the opportunity to slide down into the guttering, which, as if in sympathy with the roof, sagged wearily.

Obviously then, there was no escaping the fact that the cottage was in a sorry state of repair. It was therefore surprising that, for reasons unknown, the doors and the downstairs windows of the ruin had recently been sealed up. This had been done with modern concrete blocks, and judging by the mortar splattered everywhere, also done in some haste. The rumour in the village was that it was not so much to keep people out, as to keep something *in*. If so, it hadn't worked, because even *more* recently, a large hole had been knocked through the gable wall on the east side of the cottage. Who, or what, had done this, was a bit of a mystery.

Terry had been returning home across the fields at the end of a perfect May evening, when out of the blue (literally), a crow had tumbled from the sky and landed at his feet. An upturned gawpy eye blinked once, and then held still. The bird lay motionless on the dew soaked grass, its glossy black plumage shining like a jewel in the twilight. Terry could see that it was completely dead.

When something lands suddenly at your feet, you can't help but look up. When Terry did this, he saw a goshawk hovering just above his head. Its broad wings swept silently back and forth in perfect rhythm, and Terry was transfixed. Most people go a whole lifetime without seeing a goshawk in the wild, so to get that close to one when you were just twelve years old was quite something – at least, Terry thought it was.

With practised ease, the bird swooped down to ground level and glided into the leafy gloom of Crow Wood. Goshawks, being skilful fliers, can enter heavy undergrowth at high speed if necessary. This particular specimen, however, seemed to be in no special hurry. Terry had watched intently as it disappeared into the foliage of an elegant beech tree. Then, naturally enough, he had followed it.

So then, this was how he had been enticed deep into the wood, while the night gathered around him. The bird would allow him to approach each time to within a few metres, then slip nonchalantly off its perch and continue its journey. From beech to oak, across clearings thick with fresh green bramble, boy pursued bird with single-minded determination. He did pause just once, in a dusky thicket full of stillness. *This is a bad idea,* he told himself. It made no difference – the goshawk had him spellbound. Ignoring his own warning, he pressed onwards, and deeper into the wood.

All around, the air was rich with the gorgeous night-time scents of the woodland flowers. Foxgloves poked proudly up through the nettles, and bluebells huddled shyly in amongst the bracken. There was just a sort of *feeling* that something big was about to happen. Terry didn't notice – he only had eyes for the goshawk. He managed to keep sight of it, right up until the moment it disappeared – through the large hole in the gable wall of the Huntsman's Cottage.

At this point, he did at least do some serious consideration:

This goshawk is behaving very strangely.
Plus, it's really quite dark now.
Also plus, woods are spooky at night time – especially this one.

The sensible thing to do was fairly obvious. Terry did not, however, do the sensible thing. He stood like a statue amongst the trees, his eyes never shifting from the hole in the gable wall. And time seemed to stand still with him. Underneath the lower branches, even the mad dancing of the midges had momentarily ceased. Everything seemed to just....., stop.

Quite how long Terry stood there, he had no idea, but when a large moth fluttered across his face, he was startled out of his trance. The goshawk had not re-emerged, so albeit with his heart hammering on his chest, he did what he had to do. He stepped through the hole in the wall and into the dark enclosure of the ruined cottage. It took a moment for his eyes to become accustomed to the deeper darkness inside, but when they did, he did not find the goshawk. He did, however, find something else – something very peculiar indeed.

He was standing in what had once been the old kitchen. To his left, a rotting door through to the living room hung partly off its hinges, and slightly ajar. On the wall opposite him, stood a marble hearth and fireplace. Above this, on the middle of a decaying mantelpiece, lay a small black velvet bag. Terry noticed it immediately. He also noticed that there were fresh footprints on the concrete floor, leading over to the mantelpiece, and then back into the other room. They looked *very* fresh.

Terry felt the hair rising on the back of his neck – he had a feeling somebody was watching him from the shadows of the next room. *I should go*, he thought, but the temptation to see what was inside the bag was irresistible. He quickly crossed over to the mantelpiece and picked it up. As he did so, he became aware of something moving behind him. It was not, as he first supposed, the goshawk. It was nothing like the goshawk. To start with, it was shaped like a doughnut (only bigger), and was gold coloured. Also, it was spinning, quite fast. Then, as he watched, it rose up from the ground and hovered before him, completely unsupported. Like an insect stirred to anger, it started to hum menacingly.

Terry happened to know that the correct name for a solid such as this was a *torus*, although that fact wasn't foremost in his mind at the time. As he started to back away with growing alarm, it began to cast a sickly yellow light onto the damp and crumbling kitchen walls. The light seemed to slither along the surfaces, pursuing itself around the four corners of the room in a sort of hypnotic dance.

'*You have the Hawk's Eye.*'

Terry nearly jumped out of his skin at the sound of a voice. It wasn't that it was particularly loud or unpleasant – it was just rather unexpected. He wasn't sure where the voice was coming from, but he had an unpleasant suspicion that it might be from the next room. So, rather belatedly, he took the decision to run for his life. The trouble was, his escape was cut off by the torus. Also, there was something wrong with the air – it had become kind of sticky.

'*This is the first stone. There are six more.*'

The voice was not threatening, just calm and matter-of-fact, like an announcement at a train station. It even had a familiar sound to it. Not that that made any difference – Terry was petrified. He tried to get away, but it was like being in a swimming pool filled with treacle. It took an enormous effort just to move his arm slightly. The spinning torus was swirling the thickening air around it, and the current was beginning to drag him with it. In no time at all he was lifted off his feet, and with mounting panic, he realised that a whirlpool had formed. The torus was sucking him down into its centre.

'You cannot return until you have the seven tumblestones.'

Of course he struggled, but the situation was hopeless. He wished now he had not followed the goshawk into the wood. All he wanted was to be climbing over his back garden fence, and walking up to the comforting lights of his house. If only he could rush inside and tell his Mum that he had found a duck's nest down by the river, that there were seven olive green eggs in it, that he would never go into Crow Wood at night by himself again, that... . Unfortunately, he knew that he wasn't going to get the chance to say any of these things. Not for a while at least.

The torus had swollen to the size of a tractor tyre, and the air was pouring down through its centre like a golden liquid, spinning Terry around at dizzying speeds as it carried him with it. It must have been some kind of reflection, or maybe the light was bending in a weird sort of way. Whatever the reason, the last thing he saw as he was swallowed by the vortex, was his own startled face, looking down on him from above.

Catwalks and Canals

'How old are you?'

The boy asking the question was sitting cross-legged on the floor, in the middle of a plain woollen rug. He looked to be several years younger than Terry. He had short dark hair, and a rather flat face with mischievous eyes. His clothes were unusual – light brown breeches with a tasselled tunic to match – Terry thought perhaps it was a fancy dress costume.

'I am nine,' continued the boy, and then after some hesitation added, 'nearly.'

Terry looked around and found himself in a room with a wooden floor, wooden walls and a wooden ceiling. There was one window, quite high up, and sunlight was streaming through it onto a thick pine table and four stubby chairs. He thought maybe he was in a log cabin of some sort, but he had no idea how he had got there.

Before Terry could answer, a girl's voice came from an adjoining room.

'Polka? Stop talking to yourself and come and help me with the chores.'

The small boy scowled. 'That is my sister,' he said without enthusiasm. 'Now she will come through and discover you.' Sure enough, after a slight delay, a girl of about Terry's age appeared in the doorway. She wore a fawn coloured dress that was decorated with leather tassels, turquoise beads and white feathers. On her feet she had cedar coloured moccasins. Her long, coal-black hair fell straight over her shoulders, and reminded Terry of the shiny black plumage of the crow. She was very pretty.

For quite a long time, none of them spoke. Then the girl, all the time keeping her eyes fixed on Terry, said softly and cautiously 'Who is this, Polka?'

'I don't know yet,' he replied, 'I'm still trying to find out how old he is.'

The girl regarded Terry with a mixture of hope and wariness. Still she said nothing directly to him, so he felt he needed to volunteer some information.

'My name is Terry. I'm twelve.'

Polka gave a satisfied nod, as if an important formality was now completed.

'How did you come here?' asked the girl.

'I don't know. I was going home. There was a goshawk, and a gold spinning thing.' This information had an electrifying effect on the girl. Her eyes shone with excitement, and eagerly she came over and sat down neatly next to her younger brother.

'I knew it,' said Polka calmly, 'I knew it when he fell out of the air.'

'I am Meeshka,' said the girl, 'and this is my brother Polka. He is very clever.'

'Where are we?' asked Terry.

'This building belongs to Hev and Gwen. We have not met Hev yet, but Gwen is nice. She is looking after us. Perhaps she will help you too.'

'I just want to go home. What is this place called?'

'This city is called Carthag. I do not know where it is, but things are different here. It is difficult to explain.'

'Do you come from our land?' asked Polka suddenly. He regarded Terry's jeans, trainers and football shirt with the number seven on the back. 'You don't look like you do.'

'I come from Amesbury, near Salisbury.'

Meeshka and Polka looked at him blankly.

'You know – near Stonehenge?'

They shook their heads.

'Well surely you've heard of England? Or the United Kingdom?'

'We have not heard of any of these places,' replied Meeshka sorrowfully. 'I think perhaps that you come from a different world to ours.'

'What do you mean?' asked Terry.

'Well,' began Meeshka, 'Gwen thinks that perhaps our home is in another world, and…'

'I understand it better,' said Polka interrupting. 'In our world, we have horses, not these strange morsk creatures, and we don't have cities made of towers like this. A lot of things are the same though, like the bighorns and the chickens.'

Terry listened to all of this carefully. He walked over to the window, and by standing on tip-toe, he was able to see out. He got a bit of a surprise.

To start with, the room they were in was quite high up,

in what seemed to be a tall wooden tower. There were lots of these towers all around, most of them linked by long catwalks – crooked planks suspended from ropes. Every tower had a ground floor of whitewashed stone that formed a foundation, but the upper storeys were invariably constructed from wood. Each tower was connected to others, at various levels, like a giant three dimensional spider's web. Terry could see that it would be possible to travel long distances across the city, without ever needing to go down to ground level.

Looking further afield, he could see what was either a very straight river, or a canal. Colourful boats were being towed by creatures that appeared, as far as he could tell from that distance, to be some kind of reindeer.

'I don't recognise this place at all,' he said, 'not even from TV.'

'TV?' asked Meeshka innocently.

'You don't have TV?'

'Is TV a place?'

'No, no. It's something you watch. Don't you have computers then? And internet? What about mobiles?'

Meeshka shrugged hopelessly. 'There is so much we don't understand.'

'I would like to know more about TV and these other things,' announced Polka.

Terry sat down and held his head in confusion. 'Wait a minute. I'm going to say some words, and you just say yes when you recognise any of them.' Meeshka and Polka nodded politely.

Terry thought carefully, and then began. 'London, USA, Pacific Ocean, Chocolate, Aeroplane, Moon.'

'Yes!' said Meeshka and Polka together.

'Of course we know the Moon,' said Polka scornfully, 'Also Ocean, but not the one you said.'

Another thought occurred to Terry. 'How come you both talk English?'

'We speak Saxian,' replied Polka stubbornly. 'So do you.'

'Our people are the Camer,' explained Meeshka, 'we live in a land that we call Saxonia.'

'We were taken into this world a few days ago,' she continued. 'We too followed a hawk. It seemed injured, and it led us into a cave. There we were sucked through a spinning gold ring, just like you, and into this world. We also would like to get back to our home. Our parents will be searching for us.'

Terry nodded sympathetically. 'Did someone speak to you?' he asked, 'when you were being sucked through the gold ring?' Meeshka shook her head.

'Well they did to me. They said I could not return until I had the seven tumblestones. I didn't understand what that meant.'

'What else did they say?' asked Polka curiously.

'Nothing else much, but there were some footprints, and I found something.' Terry had remembered the black velvet bag he had picked up off the mantelpiece in the ruined cottage. He searched in his pocket and found it there. Undoing the drawstring, he emptied the contents onto the rug, and Meeshka and Polka gathered round eagerly. There was a single smooth stone – a tumblestone. Shades of amber and deep, dark green swirled from beneath the shining glassy surface. It was like looking into the depths of a beautiful eye.

There was also a torn piece of paper, with a short verse, hand-written upon it.

Crack the riddle, find the stone
Read the winning place alone
Only take a single sign
Set together in a line

Seek the Watcher, fear the foe
Burn the riddle once you know
On the journey, trust in few
Watcher watches out for you

Terry read the verse aloud, and then read it again to himself. 'What is that supposed to mean?' he asked blankly.

'We need to find someone called the Watcher,' replied Polka confidently. 'They are waiting for us.' Terry nodded in agreement, wondering who the foe might be.

'That is not all,' continued Polka as he stared thoughtfully at the verse. 'There is another message here.'

'What is it, Polka?' asked Meeshka with interest.

'I don't know yet. But I will solve it.'

Meeshka smiled hopefully at Terry. 'Polka is good at things like this,' she said. 'And Gwen will help us when she returns. She has gone to talk to her husband, Hev. He is working on the canals. She says that he will know more about what has happened, and why we have been brought here. They also speak our language in this land, although it is not called Saxian. Gwen calls it Eurasian.'

'Well lots of other countries speak English,' said Terry, 'but if they don't have TV here then it can't be the same world that I come from. Just about everyone has TV.'

'What is this TV?' asked Polka, looking up from the verse he was studying. Before Terry could reply, they heard the sound of someone running up stairs below them. A door in the corner of the room was flung open and a young woman appeared. She had straw-coloured hair and bright blue eyes, and wore a white cotton dress tied with a black cord at the waist. Terry guessed she was about thirty. In fact, she was twenty-six.

'Meeshka! Polka! Come quickly! The Bandero are coming for you!'

She suddenly noticed Terry. 'Who is that?' she asked suspiciously.

'Oh Gwen, his name is Terry,' answered Meeshka excitedly. 'He came here the same way that we did.'

'Only from a different world,' added Polka.

'Can we help him too?' implored Meeshka.

'Yes,' said Gwen hesitatingly, 'yes of course, but we must leave immediately – they are only minutes behind.'

Hurriedly, Terry gathered up the stone and paper from the rug. He put them back into the black velvet bag, and returned it safely to his pocket.

Gwen came into the room and rushed over to the window to look down. 'They are here already. Quickly now, we must cross over the corsa, on the next floor up.' She flung open a large trunk under the window, and frantically rummaged inside, removing three grey blankets. 'You must put these around you to hide your clothes, else all of Carthag will notice us leaving.'

The three children draped the blankets around themselves as best they could, and followed Gwen out of the room and into a sort of stairwell, formed by a series of trapdoors and ladders.

'Who are the Bandero?' Terry asked Meeshka, as they climbed the steps one by one.

'I don't know,' she said, 'but Gwen will know what to do.'

'Perhaps they are the foe,' said Polka sombrely.

They moved up through a trapdoor in the ceiling of the stairwell, and then into a room on the floor above. It had no furniture at all – just creaking floorboards. There was a single door in the opposite wall, and when Gwen opened it a whistling wind rushed in. All Terry could see at first was bright blue sky. Then he realised there was a gangway onto one of the precarious catwalks that formed a bridge over to another tower.

'Quietly now!' whispered Gwen, as she peered cautiously over the edge. 'We must wait until they are in the building.'

Down below in the street, three men dressed in dark green tunics and blue capes had arrived. They were riding what appeared to Terry to be most peculiar animals. The grey coated body of the creatures was identical to that of a horse, but elaborate antlers reached back almost to the saddles that were strapped to their backs. The three men dismounted and questioned someone walking in the street below, who nodded and pointed to the tower they were in.

'They have found us,' whispered Gwen tensely, 'get ready to cross the corsa.' Tethering their beasts by a halter that hung loosely under the neck, the three Bandero slipped quietly into the white stone building beneath.

'Good! They have not left a guard outside,' Gwen told them. 'Come now, children – onto the corsa. It will feel strange at first, but just hold tight to the rope on both sides, and place your feet in the middle of each plank.' Gwen went ahead, followed first by Polka and then Meeshka. Terry came last of all. The corsa was constructed from single planks bound together by rope, tied through holes at each end. It swayed alarmingly as they stepped onto it, and Terry was conscious of the sickening drop below them. A strong breeze was rocking the corsa to and fro, making it difficult for the children to keep their balance. Meeshka walked hesitatingly, and with obvious discomfort. She paused frequently, screwing her eyes tight shut to avoid looking at the drop below. Terry tried to make encouraging comments from behind, but in truth he was finding it equally difficult, even though he generally had a good head for heights. He found himself gripping the rope on each side very tightly, and he had to force his eyes to focus on the tower opposite.

Gwen was well-practised at using the catwalks, and rapidly made it over to the next tower, where she had to wait anxiously for the children to catch up. Polka, being lighter, moved fairly confidently over the swaying planks, and was not far behind her. Meeshka, however, was much slower and took nearly a minute to cross the short distance, with Terry close behind.

'We must hurry,' said Gwen urgently. The second tower had another corsa on the same level, forming a right-angle with the one they had just crossed. This stretched over to a further tower, but when they reached this they had to climb down a ladder inside in order to reach the next corsa. All the time, Gwen cast worried glances back up towards her own tower, fearing the three Bandero would suddenly appear at the gangway and see them making their escape.

So they progressed from tower to tower. Sometimes they had to climb up or down several storeys in order to reach the particular corsa Gwen wished to take. The stairwells in each tower were treated as communal passages, used by all, and occasionally they would have to wait as other people came up or down a particular ladder. Some would greet Gwen warmly, but no remark was made about the three strangers that huddled in their blankets by her side.

Before long, they had left their own tower far behind, and Terry could see that Gwen was leading them gradually down towards the ground. As they emerged from the white stone base of a final tower, they found themselves on a quiet backstreet, and finally Gwen slowed the pace.

'Well done, children,' she said, 'now we must head for the canal jetty, and hope that we meet no Bandero. We need to get you all different clothes to wear as soon as possible. You cannot be always travelling with blankets draped around you.' They set off, walking calmly down the dusty street, doing their best not to attract attention.

'Hev will be waiting with the boat,' Gwen continued. 'We must smuggle you out of Carthag tonight. All the Bandero will be looking for you.'

'Who are these Bandero?' asked Terry.

Gwen turned and regarded him for a while before answering.

'They are the Baron's secret police, and there are very many of them. Baron Hart commands this division of the Realm, and is tasked to keep order. In truth, he is simply a pawn of Emperor Cahito, but the Emperor seldom ventures this far north these days.' Gwen frowned pensively before adding 'the Baron can be very cruel, if crossed.'

'Why are his Bandero looking for us?' asked Polka.

'That is a good question. I do not know for sure. My husband has heard tales from merchants in the south. Rumours that important strangers would come here – young people, with strange clothes and customs. Hev also heard that these strangers would have some possession, or perhaps information, that the Baron greatly desires. Something he would happily kill for.'

'Are we then these strangers?' asked Meeshka.

'Again, I do not know for sure, but I think perhaps you might be. In any case, word has reached the Bandero of your arrival at my tower. Some neighbour, I think, with a loose tongue or an eye for some profit. Hev was able to warn me they were on your trail. That is why I rushed home to you, but maybe I was followed.'

As they moved north through the city, the high towers were becoming less common, replaced by two or three storey terraces of a design more familiar to Terry. What struck him most was that there were no cars or bikes. Only wooden carts pulled by either big horned cattle or else the strange horses with antlers. It felt as if he had been transported back in time. They passed a blacksmith, standing in his apron over a glowing forge, wielding a large pair of tongs. He gave them a casual glance as they passed, but like most people they saw, he seemed pre-occupied with his own affairs. Others they passed in the street nodded politely, but nobody bothered them.

At each street corner, Gwen paused and carefully checked for any sign of the Bandero, before allowing them to proceed.

'How much further,' asked Polka, 'my feet are hurting.'

'We are almost there,' answered Gwen. 'At this next corner you will wait behind the barrels until I come for you. I must check that our boat is clear.'

The children did as they were asked, crouching down out of sight. They could smell the canal already – a dank mixture of mouldy wood and water weed. As they waited, a brown hairy mongrel with only one eye wandered aimlessly down the street. Noticing the children behind the barrels, it stopped to sniff around them with interest. Meeshka raised an arm to stroke it, but it gave a low menacing growl, so she quickly withdrew her hand. After satisfying itself that the children had no food to offer, it trotted off and disappeared around the corner of the street.

'This is very different to where I live,' said Terry quietly.

'It is different to our village in the forest also,' said Meeshka ruefully.

'What are the people here like?' asked Terry.

'Gwen is very nice,' replied Meeshka. 'We have not really met anyone else much.'

'Did you just appear in Gwen's tower like I did?'

'No. Gwen found Polka and I asleep in a big crate by the market. She took us home with her that night.'

'There were apples in the crate,' added Polka, 'but they were shaped like pears.' He nodded, as if this were somehow significant.

'Polka has noticed that some things in this world are slightly different to the things in our world,' explained Meeshka.

'Like the horses with antlers?' asked Terry.

'Yes. Other things too.'

It was not long before Gwen returned and led them down a narrow street of buildings that had no ground floor windows. It ended abruptly by the grassy bank of a wide canal. The sun was now very low in the sky, and as the children approached the water, they cast long shadows along the towpath. To their right, a short backwater led off the main canal, and Hev's boat was moored here, on a small jetty that was attached to a forlorn-looking boathouse. At one time this building had been green, but the paint was so badly flaked now that weathered grey wood showed through everywhere.

As Gwen led them up onto the jetty, two beautiful birds, similar to swans, glided gracefully out of the boathouse. Their iridescent turquoise plumage sparkled against the carpet of green duckweed that covered the water's surface. Terry had a keen interest in wildlife, and could identify many species, but he had never seen such splendid birds as these before. Then his eye was caught by one of the horse-reindeers that grazed placidly on the bank behind the jetty.

'What are these creatures?' he asked as he cautiously approached it.

Gwen smiled. 'We call them morsk. Up here in the north, we still use them to tow the boats. Down in the south, Hev says that many of the boats have these new mechanical steam engines, but they are very noisy, and often break down.'

Terry was fascinated with the morsk. He reached out to the animal, which remained unconcerned, allowing him to touch its velvet antlers and stroke its head. In every respect, from the neck down, the morsk was a grey horse. Even the basic shape of the head was similar, but from between the ears sprouted an elaborate set of antlers which swept backwards over the neck. The eyes were also different. They were large, blue, and held a gentle expression. Terry thought they looked like something you would find in the sea.

A man suddenly poked his head up out of the boat deck.

'Quickly Gwen, before we are seen,' he said urgently. He climbed ashore and loosened the mooring rope. He was very tall, with long dark hair, and grey-green eyes that held an anxious expression.

'This is Hev,' said Gwen to the children, but the man interrupted her.

'Introductions can wait until later,' he said briskly, 'we need to get on our way.'

Meeshka nudged Terry, and reluctantly he gave the morsk a final pat and climbed aboard. Gwen ushered the children down into the hold out of sight. 'Don't worry, children,' she said, 'he will be in a better humour when we are safely out of the city.'

The boat was not like the narrow boats Terry had seen on canals back home. Those boats were generally not tall enough for an adult to stand up in comfortably. Hev's boat, however, had a hold where the cargo (fore and aft) and the sleeping quarters (mid-ships) were; a main deck section where the galley and eating quarters were located; and on the slightly raised upper deck, an open bridge section from where the boat was navigated. On the side of this was a framed plaque, proudly proclaiming the boat's name, 'Gwendoline'. Above the waterline, the vessel was painted a cheerful red, while the shutters and trapdoors were pristine white. Unlike the boathouse, the boat looked very well maintained.

Gwen took them down into the sleeping quarters, and asked them to remain hidden until darkness had descended, and the boat was clear of the city limits. She left the hatch open so they had a little light and plenty of air, but nonetheless, it was a restless wait. They listened anxiously to every sound from above, wondering each time if it were the Bandero in pursuit.

After what seemed to the children to be a very long

time, delicious cooking smells began to waft down from above, and Gwen called from up on the main deck.

'You can come up now,' she said,' but if you see another boat coming then go and hide below deck straight away. The meal will be ready shortly.'

The children sat together with their feet dangling over the towpath side of the boat, as darkening countryside drifted past beside them. The tow rope was attached to a tall mast at the prow of the boat, which kept it clear of any obstructions. The morsk was about five metres ahead, being led by a short bald man who the children had not seen when they boarded. His skin was the colour and texture of a walnut, and he turned around only once, to regard them with his piercing blue eyes.

Gwen hummed happily to herself in the galley, and Hev was up on the bridge, holding the tiller wheel and staring resolutely ahead into the gathering gloom. As the first star winked in the twilight, Meeshka pointed upwards and said 'Starlight, star so bright, first to shine on me tonight. I wish I may, I wish I might, have the wish I've wished tonight.'

Terry looked at her in surprise. 'Why did you say that?' he asked.

'It is just a rhyme that the children of my land sometimes say,' replied Meeshka carelessly.

'But children in *my* land also say that, or something very similar,' said Terry earnestly. 'That is the first thing about your world that sounds familiar. Perhaps it is not so different from my world, even if you don't have T.V.'

'That is interesting,' agreed Meeshka thoughtfully. 'We need to learn more about our different lands.'

'I know what you wished for,' interrupted Polka childishly.

'Oh Polka, you should know not to speak of that,' admonished his sister, 'don't you want my wish to come true?'

'Not just yet,' replied Polka, 'this new land is too exciting.'

Gwen poked her head out of the galley. 'Our meal is ready now. Come and we will eat. Then we will talk, for Hev has more information.'

The children were very hungry, so the meal of grilled vegetables and fish was eaten with very little interruption for conversation. There were bananas to follow, which although not very exciting to Terry, proved a delight to Meeshka and Polka, who had never come across such fruit before. When everything was cleared away, Gwen brought the cooking stove out onto the deck and the two adults and three children huddled around the warmth of its glowing embers. It was properly dark now, and there was a sudden chill in the air, so the children were glad of the blankets Gwen had given them in the tower.

'It is time to talk,' said Hev seriously. 'Although Gwen has told me what she knows about you, we have not been properly introduced. My name is Hev, and I work the canals, transporting goods between traders. I have been down in Sudin, and have just returned to Carthag this morning.' Meeshka and Polka stood up and, placing their palms together between their eyes, bowed courteously. 'To meet you is our honour,' said Meeshka politely. Terry realised that something was expected of him, so he stood up and offered his hand to Hev, who shook it solemnly.

'Thank you for helping us,' Terry said awkwardly, and then sat down again. Hev nodded seriously, and Gwen smiled.

'I will tell you what I have learnt over the last few days,' continued Hev, 'but you three must think carefully, and tell us all that you know too.'

Hev stoked the cooking embers, and seemed to be thinking carefully before he began.

'I cannot promise you that what I have heard is the truth, although I have heard the same tale from different sources. Nor can I say for certain that it has anything to do with the three of you. Still, your strange clothes and different ways make me believe that you must be connected somehow to the story the merchants have given me.' Gwen nodded in agreement, the red embers of the stove glowing in her eyes.

'About twenty years ago,' continued Hev, 'a traveller came to this land. He was not like other people. He wore a hooded cloak and kept largely to himself. He stayed a while, and then disappeared. I do not remember him, but Gwen thinks perhaps she met him once.' The children looked expectantly at Gwen.

'Yes,' she agreed, 'I feel sure it was the same person. I was very young, perhaps only five or six. At that time, we were living in a small village many miles to the north of here. My mother had asked me to fetch a small pail of water from the well. The stranger was standing nearby, staring at me. I remember he removed the hood of his cloak and smiled at me. He spoke briefly, but I do not remember what he said. I think perhaps it was something I did not understand. I was frightened and ran home with the water, spilling much of it on the way. My mother scolded me for my carelessness. I only saw the stranger that one time.'

'How is this person connected to us?' asked Terry.

'The rumour is that the traveller came here for a purpose. Not to seek something, but to leave something. Nobody could say for sure, but one story had it that the stranger possessed some stones that have a mysterious power.'

Meeshka looked excitedly at Terry. 'Remember what the hawk said to you.'

'What is this?' asked Hev quickly.

'I don't think it was the hawk, it was just a voice from somewhere,' explained Terry, 'but as I was taken from my world, it said to me I must find the seven tumblestones. I could not return until I had the seven tumblestones.'

'What are these stones you speak of?' asked Hev. Terry removed the black bag from his pocket once again, and took out the tumblestone and verse. Hev and Gwen both gasped when they saw the beautiful gleaming stone.

'Can this truly be one of the special stones the tales speak of?' asked Hev, his eyes opened wide in wonder.

'Well I suppose it is,' replied Terry, 'because the voice told me that I had the Hawk's Eye, the first stone. It said I had to find the other six before I could return.'

'What is written on the paper?' asked Gwen. Terry showed her and Hev the verse, and Gwen read it aloud.

Crack the riddle, find the stone
Read the winning place alone
Only take a single sign
Set together in a line

Seek the Watcher, fear the foe
Burn the riddle once you know
On the journey, trust in few
Watcher watches out for you

'Polka thinks there is a secret message in the poem,' explained Meeshka, 'but we do not know who this Watcher might be.'

Hev read the verse again, looking very thoughtful. 'I think perhaps, that I do,' he said.

'Hev?' asked Gwen in surprise. Hev looked across at her and nodded.

'The traveller disappeared for a while,' he began, 'shortly after he first arrived here. But he came back about a month later. I have heard that he spent this time with someone called the Watcher. That name was repeated to me only last week, but their connection to the traveller is unclear. The story goes that they guard the pass through the mountains in the north – at a place known as the Ravine of Silence.'

'For what purpose?' asked Gwen.

'People say that they simply watch, and wait for something, or perhaps someone.'

'That must be the same person as in the poem!' said Meeshka excitedly.

'We must be cautious,' warned Hev, 'but I think it is probably so.'

'How far away is the Ravine of Silence?' asked Polka sleepily. He was struggling to keep awake by the warm cooking stove.

'Perhaps eight to ten days by morsk. It is a long way.'

'What happened to the traveller?' asked Meeshka

'By the time he returned to these parts, the Baron had picked up news of him – especially the part about the stones of power. That is the present Baron's father, you understand. He is dead now, killed in some battle to the south. In any case, it was not long before the Bandero found the traveller and imprisoned him in Castle Turuk. From there, the trail goes cold. Some people say that the traveller escaped, but if you ever get to see Castle Turuk you will understand that that is most unlikely. It stands on a great rock, surrounded on all sides by a tall and powerful waterfall in the shape of a morsk-shoe. I think myself that either the traveller died attempting to escape, or was killed by the Baron.'

'But I still don't see how we fit into this story,' said Terry frowning.

'Well then, what do you make of this?' answered Hev. 'Before he was captured by the Bandero, the traveller had let it be known that many years later, new strangers would come to this land. They would be children, lost and alone. Their clothes would look strange. It was said they would need the help of all good people, for something very important would depend upon their success.'

Hev paused to let this important news sink in, before continuing. 'Now you can understand why the Bandero are searching for you. The new Baron will know all of this and more, and his heart would yearn for a stone of power. If there are *seven* stones, he will yearn *seven* fold.'

'Why is that man listening to us?' asked Polka suddenly. The others had thought Polka had dropped off to sleep, but he had been watching the man leading the morsk. This man had gradually been edging further back in the darkness, straining to hear the conversation in the boat.

'What is this Mozz?' asked Hev angrily, 'return to your tow beast.'

'I meant no offence by it, I'm sure,' replied the man sulkily, disappearing back into the gloom up ahead to lead the morsk.

'Can we trust him?' asked Gwen anxiously.

'I have used him many times,' replied Hev thoughtfully. 'He is a strange one, right enough. He keeps his own counsel, and often disappears from the canals for weeks at a time. But I think he is probably just curious – as many others will be.'

'No doubt,' Gwen nodded, 'the first priority is to get the children well away from Carthag. Then we must decide what to do.'

'Well then, it is time to sleep,' said Hev with finality. 'We will see what tomorrow brings. Good night to you, children.' The children said their goodnights, and Gwen led them down into the hold of the boat. She pulled some straw mattresses from a trunk for them to sleep on.

'These are a little dusty, I'm afraid,' she said apologetically, 'but they are dry and comfortable. Sleep well, and try not to worry.'

'Why are you helping us?' asked Meeshka. 'It could be dangerous for you and Hev.'

Gwen smiled. 'You were not sent to another – you were sent to me. I do not understand why this was so, but I know it was for a reason. For good or bad, our fates are tied to yours now, little one. We will not abandon you.'

As he settled down, Terry could not help wishing he was safely home in his own bed. He expected he would lie awake for hours worrying about how he was ever going to get back to his own world, but he was so tired that he fell into a dreamless sleep within a few moments.

When he woke again, he could see that it was still dark. At first he could not remember where he was, but someone was shaking his arm. And a voice was whispering urgently.

27

'Terry! Terry! Wake up! The Bandero are searching the boats up ahead!'

Castle Turuk

Captain Tache rode through the night in order to reach
Castle Turuk before dawn. Leaving Carthag around dusk, he
paused only once, to rest and water his morsk at a spring-
hole clearing, deep in the middle of the forest. The
well-worn trail from Carthag to the castle was wide and
properly maintained, and with a full moon shining brightly
over the treetops, he was able to press on at best speed. The
captain had much to think about as he rode alone through
the darkness – not least, the matter of how he was going to
explain to Baron Hart that the children (all *three* of them, it
now appeared) had eluded his men so far. The captain was a
brave and loyal soldier, but he did not relish the forthcoming
interview in the Baron's stronghold. Nevertheless, this caused
no lessening of his pace. As a Bandero captain, he would do
his duty, and report the facts accurately.

Just as the moon was sinking wearily over the forest canopy, the huge dark silhouette of the imposing castle materialised out of the night sky. At the same moment, the awesome roar of the Falls of Turuk became audible above the hoof beats of his galloping morsk. For most of his journey, tall firs had stood like stern statues on either side of him. Now though, they began gradually to thin out, as if a part of the darkness itself were dissolving away. Then the last tree was behind him, and Captain Tache emerged from the vast forest. He reined in his morsk, and cautiously guided it out onto the rocky plateau that surrounded the great falls. Here he paused, and standing in his stirrups, he took a moment to survey the legendary scene. Even by the half-light of pre-dawn, and even though he had seen it many times before, and even though he was exhausted, the sight was still breathtaking.

Castle Turuk was built on a rocky prominence, standing on an island, surrounded by the sweeping arc of the Falls of Turuk. The castle was more or less moulded onto the rock, so there was no clear line to observe between natural stone and castle stone. The falls formed almost a complete circle around the castle, leaving only a narrow gorge down which the raging torrent drained. The waters around the island were kept in constant turmoil, so that even if a vessel survived its passage up the gorge, fighting an impossible current, there would be no hope for it once it reached the cauldron's bowl. The river water dropped fifty metres into this bowl on all sides, and even in high summer the volume of water was sufficient to sink the sturdiest of crafts. Consequently, the only access to the castle was by a narrow suspension bridge. This was slung from the small promontory of dry stone slab at the head of the gorge. It stretched tightly out over the raging waters and across to a gatehouse, built into the castle's sheer southern wall. Around the forest end of this bridge, several service buildings of the castle were clustered, including the stables, granary, barracks and some livestock byres.

On arriving at this outer complex, Captain Tache went straight to the stables to have his morsk tended to. Here he had to find and waken the sleepy night groom, who had left his post for the comfort of the hay loft several hours earlier, little dreaming a Bandero captain would be arriving to disturb his slumber. Tache soon had the young lad hopping to his duty, with dire threats of the consequences if his morsk were not well looked after. It was impossible to take a morsk over to the castle, for none could negotiate the suspension bridge – the alarming way it swayed under any weight, together with the deafening roar of the falls on all sides, was certain to panic any beast and result in the loss of both morsk and rider.

Once he was satisfied that his morsk would be made comfortable, Captain Tache spoke briefly to the bridge guards, then crossed over to the castle as dawn broke behind him. Having left word of his arrival at the gatehouse, he headed directly to his personal quarters, situated in a suite of rooms just off the south bailey. Hoping that the Baron would rise late and take breakfast before interviewing him, he collapsed onto his damp mattress and fell immediately asleep, still in full battle dress. However, after just a few precious minutes, he was rudely awakened by the Baron's personal valet, and told to report to the Map Room immediately.

Baron Hart stared at his divisional captain in a cold

calculating way. To Captain Tache, the Baron's stare felt much like he imagined a sword passing through his eye-socket would feel. He still stood to attention, as he had been doing since he entered the Map Room five minutes earlier. The Baron had not yet seen fit to put him at ease. Tache's dark curly hair suggested a man of fewer years than his thirty-five, but his weathered complexion and experienced gaze told the truth. He was not particularly tall, but his broad frame gave the impression of both strength and weight. His green tunic was stained dark with sweat, but he had gathered his black cape of captaincy tightly around his shoulders, to hide what he could of the rigours of his long ride. He did his best to meet the Baron's cold stare unflinchingly. Most interviews with the Baron tended to be uncomfortable affairs, and this one seemed to be going just as badly as the captain had anticipated.

'I want both these children in the castle by sundown tomorrow,' said the Baron in a cold tone that left no room for negotiation.

'Sir, my latest report suggests there may be a third child,' replied Captain Tache tersely. He felt it was good policy to talk tersely to the Baron — any sign of weakness and you were in trouble. Nevertheless, he could not hide the beads of sweat on his forehead.

'What's this, Tache? From where has this third child come?'

'We have not confirmed that yet, sir. We raided the safe-tower that the two children were known to be using, but they had left already. Interrogation of people in neighbouring towers would suggest they had been joined by a third child. They were seen leaving the building with the woman, the three children draped in blankets.'

'Blankets?'

'Sir, we conclude this was an attempt to hide their strange appearance.'

The Baron nodded thoughtfully. 'But what of the Augury?' he asked pointedly. 'It speaks only of the *one* child.'

'Yes, sir, but my men were very clear on this point. The woman *does* have three children with her. It is our belief that none of them are native to Carthag.'

The Baron was tall and heavily built. His dark greasy black hair fell limply against an equally dark and greasy beard, so it was impossible to see where hair finished and beard began. His nose was very slightly crooked, but beneath the beard, a strong jaw line was concealed. Were it not for his ferociously bushy black eyebrows, he would have been a handsome man. He gathered his dark red cloak around him against the early morning chill, and studied the map in front of him for a while.

The Map Room was well-named. It was dominated by a large square table on which, in perfectly polished marquetry, a map of the lands around Castle Turuk had been inlaid. This stretched from the mountains in the north to the ocean in the south – from the vast forest in the west, to Carthag in the east – which lay on the border of the Wetlands. Pearl insets marked the important towns. More distant lands continued on the walls of the room, etched into the wood panelling and expertly highlighted in a soot-black ink.

Being deep down in the centre of what was an unusually large keep, the Map Room was windowless, and lit by great candle chandeliers hung from the ceiling. Occasionally, an unsecured candle would lean beyond its spill-guard and deposit molten tallow on the table below.

Removing these greasy droplets with a fingernail was a constant preoccupation of the Baron.

'How did these strangers come to Carthag?' he pondered, more to himself than the tired officer still standing to attention before him. 'Unseen by all in their travels, suddenly they are there, in the heart of the city. How can this be?'

'We will answer these riddles when they are apprehended, sir, I promise you.'

The Baron stroked his beard thoughtfully. 'When you find them I want them searched, Tache. All possessions must be collected and brought here without delay. Do it personally, or if not, your most trusted man, and the swiftest morsk. Report directly to me – do you understand?'

'Completely, sir.'

'Good. What strength of men are engaged in the search?'

'Two full complements directly, sir, but orders have been passed down to the entire rank of Bandero to be watchful and report the movement of any strangers.'

'And the woman sheltering the children?'

'Of no previous account, sir. The wife of a boater, who trades with merchants in the south.'

'She cannot be of no previous account!' said the Baron with obvious exasperation, 'something has been missed.'

Captain Tache was about to deny this, but caught the unpleasant glint in the Baron's eye and changed his mind. 'Our enquiries will continue,' he said, clearing his throat uncomfortably. 'At present it is not clear why the children came to her, but it is only a matter of time before we discover the connection. Upon my return, I shall ensure she is found and questioned at length.'

Baron Hart nodded curtly. 'Make sure you do.' He then turned to consider the map on the wall behind them, showing a large ocean that gave way eventually to a borderless continent with few marked features. 'What of Cahito's spies?' he continued, 'what do they know of this business?'

'As you know, sir, the Emperor has unrest to quell closer to home. I have no reports of any of his men operating in or around Carthag at this time. I think we may assume that news of the strangers has not yet reached him.'

'You will assume nothing where Cahito is concerned! Be vigilant!'

'Yes, sir!'

The Baron stared once more at his captain, and suddenly seemed to see him properly for the first time. As Captain Tache weathered this stare, he saw the Baron's grim features relax slightly.

'Stand at ease, Tache – you look dreadful.'

The captain responded gratefully, setting his feet apart in a more comfortable stance and relaxing his arms. Baron Hart gave a glassy smile, then adopted a gentle and patronising tone, as if speaking to a young child. 'It will pay us all to be cautious, Tache. We can not afford for Cahito to get wind of this matter. Whilst we keep good order and pay our annual tithes, Turuk will remain a distant irrelevance to the Emperor. Were he to gain any knowledge of the contents of the Augury, or worse still that the prophesied child had possibly arrived in our midst, then I can assure you his attention would prove most unwelcome to us all.'

'I understand that, sir,' nodded Tache. 'We will be, as you suggest, vigilant.'

The Baron seemed suddenly to tire, and moved

abruptly over to a large leather armchair in front of the empty fireplace. The wooden frame of the chair was ornately carved from dark oak, and intricate engravings decorated the arms and head. Unusually, the chair was constructed to swivel on an iron crosspiece base. Baron Hart sat back wearily, and swung around so as to present the back of it to his divisional captain. He began to examine his fingernails – a habit he had when he considered an interview was concluded.

'Take a couple of hours rest before your return to Carthag,' he said absently. 'You may go now.' Captain Tache snapped to attention once more, and saluted the back of the chair, feeling somewhat foolish to do so. He turned to leave, but as he reached the door of the Map Room, the Baron spoke again.

'Find me these children, Tache, and do so without delay.'

Captain Tache closed the door of the Map Room slowly and with great care, allowing the latch to close with a gentle but satisfying click. Then he struck the stone wall outside the door with considerable force, making a dull thud with his gloved fist. *Two whole hours rest!* He rather hoped the Baron had heard him expressing his frustration.

Night Games

'Quickly, children,' urged Gwen, 'there is not much time.' She held a single candle in her hand, and in the flickering gloom of the cramped hold, Terry saw that Meeshka and Polka were also stirring from their sleep.

'I have found some better clothing for you all amongst our cargo. It may not fit so well, but it will be safer for you. Change now in the shadows.'

Terry found he had been given grey leather trousers and waistcoat, with a white collarless shirt and leather sandals. The clothes smelt a bit musty but weren't too bad a fit. He was reluctant to abandon his trainers for the leather sandals, which looked uncomfortable, but he knew that this was necessary. He hoped to retrieve them later, when they had escaped the Bandero. Meeshka and Polka had hessian jerkins and trousers, but retained their moccasin footwear. Polka grumbled a little that everything was too big for him, but after Meeshka quietly admonished him, he quickly changed. When they were ready, Gwen gathered them around her.

'We are at the intersection of two canals,' she said calmly. 'There is a system of swing-bridges here, and the Bandero have lowered them to stop all the boats. Fortunately, there are several ahead of us, and Hev has gone up to the checkpoint to try and delay them further, but it will not be long before it is our turn to be searched.'

'What will we do?' asked Meeshka anxiously.

Gwen put the candle down and traced a cross on the floor of the boat to explain.

'We are here, on the west canal, heading east out of Carthag towards the canal junction. We need to take the north canal. You children must cut across the countryside in the darkness until you come upon it. There you must wait for us. Hev and I will take the boat through the checkpoint and pick you up again, somewhere on the north canal.'

'But that means we need to be on the opposite bank,' said Terry, remembering that the morsk had been towing off their starboard side.

'That's right,' said Gwen nodding in agreement. 'I will briefly punt the boat over to the northern bank, and you must quickly jump off.'

'How will we tell which is your boat in the dark?' asked Meeshka.

'I will be on the upper deck. If I am wearing a headscarf, all is safe and you must whistle softly when we reach you. If my head is bare, something is wrong and you must make no sound as we go past. Do not worry, I will come back and find you when I can.'

'What about the man Mozz who was listening?' asked Polka. 'Will he tell the Bandero about us?'

'I don't know,' admitted Gwen, 'we can only wait to see if his heart is good. He is already up at the junction talking with the other towmen. Come now, it is time.'

Gwen blew out the candle and led them up through the hold and onto the deck. Here she lent over the side of the boat and removed a long pole from its secure fixings just below the level of the main deck. Anchoring her feet on the right side of the boat, she placed the pole against the southern bank and pushed with all her might. Slowly the big boat drifted silently out into the centre of the canal. Gwen tugged forcefully on the pole to dislodge it from the bankside mud, and crossed quickly over to the other side. Unfortunately, there was not quite enough slack in the towrope, and the other end was still attached to a large heavy morsk. After an initial grunt of surprise, it stubbornly stood its ground, and the stern of the boat began to swing outwards.

'Gwen!' whispered Meeshka urgently, 'we are turning sideways!'

The tow rope was now taut, and the bow of the boat was held midstream. Unfortunately, the momentum from Gwen's punt had carried the stern over and almost up to the northern bank. This put the boat in an unusual position, likely to draw the attention of the Bandero.

'If they see us...,' continued Meeshka frantically.

'You will just have to jump from the back of the boat,' replied Gwen reassuringly. Her voice was soft and calm, but sweat was streaming down her brow.

'OK,' said Terry, moving down to the stern of the boat. 'It's close enough. I'll go first.' He climbed nimbly over the low guard rail, and leapt confidently for the bank, landing with a slight thud. He rolled quickly over into some long grass, and after a brief pause, he cautiously raised his head. To his left he could see the bright torches of the Bandero on the next boat but one. Occasionally gruff voices cut through the chill night air, barking orders at the boatmen. No-one seemed to have noticed that their boat was now positioned across the canal, so he beckoned Polka to follow him.

Polka climbed gingerly over the guard rail and paused to consider the distance to the bank. When he finally jumped, it was a brave attempt, but he did not quite make it, trailing a leg into the shallows with a loud splash. He squirmed quickly into the long grass beside Terry and both boys remained motionless. Meanwhile, Gwen and Meeshka had dived back down into the hold of the boat. For half a minute none of them moved or said anything, but nobody came back to investigate. The Bandero were conducting the search of each boat very thoroughly, and were engrossed in their task. Eventually, Meeshka's head re-appeared out of the hold, and quietly urged on by Gwen, she climbed the guard rail and jumped well, landing softly like a cat.

'Go swiftly little ones,' whispered Gwen, 'remember – I will find you.' Immediately she placed the pole in the bank and began to ease the stern of the boat back over to the southern side.

Without a word, the children moved quickly off into the dark countryside. The sky had clouded over so there was very little light to help them find a path, and the terrain was not easy. They had to pick their way through a tangled mess of gorse and shrub that snagged their clothing and made it impossible to follow a straight line. For a while they did not dare to speak, but after a few hundred metres they began to relax a little.

'We must be careful not to lose our way with no moon to guide us,' said Meeshka softly. 'There are some lights up ahead. Could that be the canal Gwen spoke of?'

'Probably,' replied Terry, 'but we better go a bit further north before we try and join it. We need to be well away from the junction, so nobody will see Gwen and Hev stop to pick us up.'

They walked in a silence that made even their footsteps on the soft dusty ground seem loud. The breeze of early evening had died down completely and it felt a little warmer under the cover of the clouds. The stillness of the air made the darkness seem very menacing, and every shadow concealed a threat. They could not resist the natural urge to hurry, so they trotted along in single file. Terry led the way, picking a route through the scattered gorse as best he could. Meeshka followed anxiously, just a few metres behind, and Polka brought up the rear. Meeshka kept glancing behind her, and she soon began to notice that Polka was falling too far behind.

'Polka!' whispered Meeshka nervously, 'we must keep together.' She slowed her pace a little so he could catch up.

'I know,' he replied quietly, 'but I think someone is following us.'

At Polka's words, both Meeshka and Terry stopped, frozen in their tracks. The only sound in the night was the distant hoot of a hunting owl. They stared into the blackness behind them, listening intently. There was only darkness, and silence.

'Are you sure, Polka?' asked Meeshka as they hurried forward once more.

'Fairly sure. Twice I heard twigs break behind us, and once I think I saw a shadow dodge behind a bush.' Terry continued to set a brisk pace. 'We must keep going,' he said. 'Pretend we don't know!'

Both Polka and Meeshka were having to put in little running steps every now and then to keep up with him, but after a short distance he suddenly stopped dead, as another thought occurred to him.

'We need to find out who it is before we get to the canal,' he said softly, 'in case we bring Hev and Gwen into a trap.'

'But what can we do?' whispered Meeshka.

'You two keep going, while I hide. I'll come up behind them,' replied Terry.

'Shouldn't we stay together?' asked Meeshka uncertainly, but Terry had already put his plan into action by darting behind a bush. 'Go on!' he whispered urgently. Meeshka and Polka stumbled ahead, unclear as to which direction they should be going in. Meeshka took the hand of her little brother, making the best guess she could.

Terry watched their shadows dissolve into the night as they pressed on. He lay on his stomach behind a small gorse bush, not even raising his head. About a minute passed with no sound, and he felt very alone. Already he was regretting splitting up from Meeshka and Polka, and he was just starting to think about getting up and following them when he heard a rustle in the darkness. Every muscle in his body grew suddenly tense, and his hands clenched the dusty ground. To his complete horror, he realised a person was standing just in front of him. He had not seen them appear, they were somehow just suddenly there. They made no attempt to move on, and seemed to be listening carefully. Terry's heart had frozen, and as the long seconds passed, he started to feel very frightened. He realised he was in a very vulnerable position, lying on the ground with the unknown assailant towering over him. He began to imagine the swift and deadly strike of a Bandero's blade, sweeping down on him from the darkness above, but none came. The person standing over him made no move at all, and Terry's next thought was to wonder if he should make a run for it.

'You young strangers should know that you have a strange scent. Easy to notice in the still night air, right enough.' For some reason, Terry could not believe that the man was actually speaking to him. He stayed completely still, just in case it was a bluff.

'Come now youngster, sit you up and talk to me. This night time game is over, and we are each discovered. You have done well.' Cautiously Terry raised his head and looked up. It was so very dark that he could not make out the man's face.

'Who are you?' he managed to stammer.

'I am your towman, Mozz by name.'

Terry sat up, and at the same time Mozz crouched down so that their heads were more or less at the same level. Terry had several pressing questions.

'Are you one of the Bandero?'

'I am not,' replied Mozz firmly.

'Well then why were you following us?'

'Because I have a message for you.'

'A message? From who?'

'From Yalyf, the stranger who came before you, many years ago.'

Terry considered this carefully in the darkness. There

was no threat in Mozz's voice – on the contrary, there was something reassuring.

'Why didn't you give us this message before? When we were on the boat?'

'Because I did not know if it was safe to speak in front of the boaters, Hev and Gwen. I was told to tell only the boy with the number seven on his back.'

'Number seven? Oh..., my football shirt.'

'All these years I have wondered what that could mean, until I saw you get onto the boat back in Carthag, when your blanket slipped for a moment. I had expected it likely meant a strange birthmark or such, but there was no mistaking it. There was the number seven on your back, as clear as the moon, and I knew that you had come at last.'

'I don't understand,' said Terry genuinely. 'How did this Yalyf person know I would come here? How could he know about my football shirt?'

'I could not say, but the message is doubtless for you.'

'Well, what is the message?'

'He bade me tell you this – do not despair in your quest. One day you will understand why you were chosen.'

'Is that all?' asked Terry in disappointment. Encouraging though this was, he had hoped for something more significant.

'Yes,' replied Mozz thoughtfully, 'though the meaning is not clear to me. He also said you must seek the help of someone who knows you are coming.'

Terry considered for a moment telling Mozz about the poem, but he was conscious of the warning within it – *on the journey, trust in few.* He decided not to mention it for the time being. Instead he asked 'Who do you think he meant?'

'I had judged you would know the answer to that, youngster. Is that not so?'

'No..., at least, not for sure.'

Even in the darkness, Terry felt the keenness of Mozz's gaze. There was a short silence, then Mozz patted him gently on the shoulder. 'Well, so be it then youngster. It is not for me to press you on that matter. I have fulfilled my promise to the stranger, made all those years ago. I reckon you should best run on now, and find your friends again. I must return to the boats before I am missed.'

'No, please wait. We don't understand anything. We don't know why we are here. Please tell me more.'

'There is no more I can tell you. Yalyf said you would come, and asked that if I should meet you, I give you that message. I wish you well youngster. Be careful who you trust, and remember what I have told you.' With that, Mozz turned quickly and left. He was swallowed up immediately by the night.

Terry realised it was pointless trying to make him stay, so he lost no time in setting off after Meeshka and Polka. The trouble was, he now had very little idea in which direction they had gone. He didn't want to call out, in case he was heard by the Bandero, but finding his friends was not going to be easy. The shrubs and gorse were getting less dense as he moved forward, and this allowed a little more light to penetrate the blackness. Still, he had nothing more than guesswork to guide him. He had wandered perhaps three hundred metres when ahead of him on the ground he saw a dark shadow. As he got closer, he realised it was three large sticks leaning together to make a small tepee. By their side, fashioned from further twigs, was an arrow head pointing slightly to the left. Terry felt confident that this could only be a sign left by his friends, and followed the direction given. After another three hundred metres, once again there was a miniature tepee, and a pointing arrow. Thus, by following the signs, he was led at last to a tree that stood alone on the edge of a large field. There was no further sign, so he moved into the shadows underneath the lower branches, and called cautiously. 'Meeshka? Polka?' From directly above his head, Meeshka and Polka suddenly dropped lightly to the ground.

'Did you see anyone?' asked Polka straight away.

'Yes, it was Mozz, the towman.'

Terry explained what had happened, and told them about the message he had been given. When he had finished he added 'by the way, that was a really good idea to leave the sticks and arrows. I would never have found you without them.'

'It was Polka's idea,' said Meeshka proudly. 'He is very clever.'

Polka grinned happily in the darkness. 'Also,' he said, 'we have found the new canal.'

Terry looked questioningly at Meeshka.

'It is true,' she nodded, 'a short distance ahead.'

'So now we must wait for Gwen,' said Polka confidently.

The three of them crept quietly up to the raised bank of the canal, and walked north along the towpath until they came upon a patch of tall reeds, growing right on the bank side. They lay down amongst these and made themselves as comfortable as they could. The clouds above broke and scattered once more, revealing a full moon, the reflection of which danced gently on the water's surface. It was eerily quiet. Every now and then, Terry would cautiously stand

and look down towards the junction, hoping to see signs of a boat travelling north. The most he ever saw though, was the occasional flicker of torchlight that seemed far off in the distance. It was impossible to tell exactly how far from the junction they had intercepted the north canal, but whatever was happening back there at the checkpoint, neither sight nor sound of it reached the waiting children. After a while, they began to feel cold, and Polka snuggled down between Meeshka and Terry to try to keep warm.

They had been waiting well over an hour before the first boat came. The towman and morsk were on the opposite bank, and the morsk was being led at a brisk pace, as if to make up for lost time. They could not tell if it was Mozz, but as the boat loomed up out of the darkness, it was obvious there was no-one on the upper deck, with or without a headscarf.

Another thirty minutes went by. None of them had spoken for some time, and Terry could see that Polka had fallen asleep. He could feel himself nodding as well when suddenly Meeshka nudged him and whispered 'Terry, another boat is coming! I think someone is standing on the upper deck!' Quickly she woke her brother, putting her hand over his mouth to warn him not to make any sound. Keeping his head as low as possible, Terry looked across to the opposite bank and was able to make out the tall thin figure of Hev, leading the morsk. He started to rise from the reeds but Meeshka pulled him back. 'Wait!' she whispered urgently.

The great bulk of the boat glided forward out of the gloom, and they clearly saw Gwen standing there. Her bare head was held high as she gazed resolutely forwards – it was the signal for danger. Terry was not sure if he imagined it, but it seemed that just as the boat passed, for a fraction of a second Gwen's eyes flickered over to where they lay concealed in the reeds. Whether she knew they were there or not, she made no sign to them. With a sickening feeling of despair, the three children sank back down into the cover of the reeds and watched the boat go past, fading quietly into the darkness beyond. It left only mocking ripples, lapping persistently against the banks of the canal.

Thunder and Lightning

'Gwen said she would find us,' said Meeshka resignedly.
'We must wait for her here.' Terry and Polka simply stared
blankly in disbelief, struggling to accept that the boat had
disappeared into the night. After a few moments, Polka
jumped to his feet and kicked the grass in stubborn
frustration. 'Why didn't Gwen stop?' he asked miserably.

'I don't know,' admitted Meeshka, 'but I *do* know that it
would be for a good reason. There is no point in us getting
upset. Gwen will come back for us.'

Terry nodded silently in agreement. He couldn't help
thinking how pleasant it would have been to be settling
down cosily into the hold of the boat, perhaps sipping a hot
drink that Gwen would have made. Instead, they were
stranded on the canal bank in the chill of a bleak dawn. The

first hints of light had crept over the eastern horizon, highlighting the distinct skyline of Carthag's tall towers in the distance. A sudden dew had formed on the grassy banks, and they found that they were now damp, as well as cold. Polka began to shiver, his teeth chattering noisily.

'You're right', sighed Terry at last, 'we'll just have to wait. But we should move away from the canal. It will be light again soon, and we can't risk being seen by the Bandero. Also, we need somewhere drier.'

'There is a field of maize quite close to the tree,' suggested Meeshka. 'It is tall and we could easily hide in it.'

'That sounds perfect,' agreed Terry.

'We must leave a sign for Gwen,' stuttered Polka, hugging himself to try and lessen his shivers.

'What sort of sign?' asked Terry cautiously, 'I don't think an arrow would be a good idea this time. The Bandero would be just as likely to find it.'

Polka thought for a while, his small symmetrical face frowning with concentration.

'We should draw a hawk in the dust, with its head pointing towards the field.'

Terry looked at him with widening eyes. 'That's a great idea!' he said enthusiastically, 'it won't mean anything to the Bandero, but Gwen or Hev will think of what we told them!'

Meeshka gazed proudly at her little brother. 'Good, Polka. You should draw the hawk.' Polka found a sharp stone and a suitable clear patch on the towpath, and set about his task. He paused frequently to examine his work, sometimes scrubbing out part of the drawing if he wasn't completely satisfied with it. Terry and Meeshka watched, and waited patiently.

'It is done,' announced Polka at last, having perused his effort from several angles.

'It's very good,' said Terry, genuinely impressed.

'Polka is clever at lots of things,' said Meeshka matter-of-factly, 'but now we must hide. It is getting light.' She turned and led them away from the towpath, back towards the tree.

The dawn was advancing rapidly, and a blood-red sky was developing ominously in the east.

'Red sky in the morning, shepherd's warning,' said Terry portentously. 'It's probably going to rain later.'

Meeshka smiled and nodded. 'In Saxonia, we say *If the dawn should bleed, then plant the seed*. But it means the same thing.'

'Well,' said Terry, 'we had better get under cover before it starts.'

Terry was aware that the land around them looked very different. In the dark, everything had seemed closer, and smaller. He had been only vaguely aware of a tall dense crop beyond the tree, but now he could see that the dusty gorse gave way to a large swathe of maize that extended to the north and west. The maize stood taller than all of them, planted in long orderly rows about a metre apart. The broad leaves splayed outwards, touching together at the tips to provide a canopy of cover.

They wandered into the field a short distance, and were immediately hidden from any prying eyes. Anyone watching might only have known they were there from the unnatural movement of the leaves above their heads, as they walked between the rows of crop.

'We should try and get some sleep,' said Terry, yawning as he spoke. 'It will be several hours, at least, before Gwen can return for us.'

Although the ground was hard and dry, they were all too tired to care. Polka and Meeshka simply lay down, curled up like a couple of cats, and fell asleep immediately. Terry, although equally tired, found it more difficult to get to sleep. He tossed and turned for a while, rolling around on the dusty earth beneath the maize, trying to find a comfortable position. He wondered what they would do if Gwen and Hev couldn't come back for them. Without them, they would be completely helpless, even just for food and shelter. Then he started to wonder if he would wake up back in Amesbury. Perhaps Gwen, Hev, Meeshka and Polka were all just part of an unusual dream. Even as he thought it, he knew it wasn't true – dreams never felt so real – the fresh smell of the crop, the way the hard ground poked into his back, and the song of the birds, as they began the dawn chorus to greet the new day. It all felt very different from a dream. As he lay listening to the birds, trying to identify which of the various chirps and chirrups were familiar to him, he finally fell into a deep and dreamless sleep.

A loud clap of thunder brought Terry suddenly awake with a jolt. The air was thick and warm, and felt as though it were somehow stretched very tight. Despite it being only midday, the dark purple clouds that towered above made it seem like dusk had fallen already. He glanced further up the row between the maize plants and saw Meeshka and Polka, clinging to each other with terrified expressions.

'It's just a thunder storm,' he said reassuringly, 'it's probably going to rain like mad in a moment.'

'What if Gwen is looking for us?' asked Meeshka suddenly. 'She will never find us in here.'

'Well, that's true,' admitted Terry, 'but we don't know if it's safe for us to be seen, so close to the canal.'

'But if it rains, the hawk will be washed away,' continued Meeshka. 'Gwen will expect us to be somewhere close to the canal bank. She will not come over here unless she sees the hawk.'

Terry considered all of this thoughtfully. He could not fault the logic of Meeshka's argument. 'OK,' he said, 'we'll go back to the canal, and see if we can find somewhere else to hide.'

As they crawled out from beneath the maize, the rain began. Gently at first, but gathering pace until it became torrential. It was soon battering the leaves of the crop until they drooped forlornly. As the raindrops hit the dry ground, little clouds of dust sprang up like a series of miniature explosions. Every drop left a dark stain of moisture that spread and joined others, soon turning the sandy soil a dark muddy brown.

Meeshka and Polka headed for the shelter of the tree, but Terry called them back. 'Not under the tree!' he shouted against the hiss of the downpour. 'Trees get hit by lightning, especially single ones like this.'

'But we'll get wet,' complained Polka.

'Better wet than frazzled,' grinned Terry. 'Come on! We'll run up the canal bank, in the direction the boat went. Let's hope the Bandero don't go out in storms!'

The rain was so intense that puddles were already forming on the ground. As they reached the canal, a fork of lightning flickered close by, like the sudden lick of a snake's tongue. They barely had time to turn towards it, when the violence of the thunderclap that followed almost knocked them to the ground. It wasn't the usual rumbling growl of thunder – it was more like a sudden explosion. For a moment they stood rooted to the spot, too shocked to move. Incredibly, the rain intensified further, splattering their heads and faces, and running into their eyes.

'We can't just stand here!' yelled Terry desperately.

'Look!' cried Meeshka suddenly. The boys followed her gaze up the towpath and saw a woman running towards them, waving one arm high above her head.

'It's Gwen!' yelled Meeshka joyfully, and took the first few faltering steps towards her. Gwen ran with a steady determination. Her yellow hair, darkened by the rain into shiny strands, danced upon her shoulders as she came.

Meeshka met her open arms with abandon, allowing Gwen to hug her and lift her off her feet. The boys stood shyly by, but their faces revealed just how pleased they were to find Gwen again.

'There is shelter a short way up the towpath!' yelled Gwen against the roaring hiss of the downpour. 'We will talk there. Follow me!'

The four of them ran through the storm for all they were worth. Even Polka managed to keep up. They soon reached the towpath on the western bank of the canal and continued northwards. After about five hundred metres they came to an empty hay barn, in a field next to the towpath. It had double doors on the canal side, which stood wide-open and inviting. They went inside and collapsed exhausted on the grassy floor. They were soaked to the skin, but very grateful to be out of the storm at last. The rain outside beat down remorselessly, turning the normally placid surface of the canal into an angry boiling torrent. The tin roof of the barn rattled loudly under the onslaught of the rain, but only the occasional drop found its way through and fell the five metres to the floor.

'I saw the hawk,' said Gwen happily, raindrops still trickling down her smiling face.

'What has happened?' asked Meeshka, 'why could you not stop last night?'

The smile dropped from Gwen's face and it was replaced by an anxious look.

'Two Bandero were on the boat last night. Somebody had told them that three children were seen boarding a boat, back in Carthag. They seemed to know that it was our boat, so we did not try to deny it. We told them that you must have run off while we went up to the junction to see what was happening. They detailed two officers to stay on board the boat for a few miles in case we had planned to pick you up again, once the boat was away from the junction. They stayed on board until we got to Trento, which is a village about three miles north of here. The boat is moored there, but oh, children – Hev has been arrested and they have taken him away for questioning.'

At this point Gwen paused, for tears had welled up in her eyes. Meeshka reached out her hand to Gwen's. 'We will help you rescue him,' she said with calm certainty.

Gwen forced a smile and gently shook her head. 'Hev would not want us to try that. He wants me to stay with you. He believes that you are here for an important reason, and we must help you to succeed. In any case, they will probably take Hev to Castle Turuk – escape from there is impossible. Hopefully they will let him go when they find out he really doesn't know where you are.'

There was a grim silence while the children absorbed this news.

'Where is Mozz?' asked Terry.

'I have not seen him since last night,' replied Gwen, 'he has disappeared, and I suspect he is to blame for Hev's arrest.'

'Maybe not,' said Terry, and he explained to Gwen how Mozz had followed them last night, and given him the message. Gwen's eyes widened with surprise as Terry told his story.

'Well,' said Gwen when he had finished, 'the involvement of Mozz was not expected. Still, his message seems to confirm what the verse says, and what we suspected already. Hev felt that this Watcher had some part to play in the mystery. Our path now is clear – we must go north to the Ravine of Silence.'

'Do you know the way?' asked Polka solemnly.

'No, not really,' said Gwen, laughing through her rain and tear-streaked face, 'but we will find the way. We will go as far north as the canal can take us, and then we shall see.'

'But surely we should try and do *something* to help Hev?' said Meeshka earnestly.

'The best way to help him is to keep you three safe and hidden. So long as the Bandero have no proof we have helped you, they will eventually release Hev. Baron Hart can be cruel, but he is usually just.'

'What about our other clothes!' exclaimed Terry suddenly. 'Did the Bandero find them?'

'Fortunately not,' replied Gwen calmly. 'I had hidden them deep in the hold, and the Bandero's search was not thorough. The clothes should be safe there for the moment.'

As they talked, the rain stopped, and a bright sun burst through the clouds, bringing with it great pools of blue sky.

Everything sparkled freshly in the brilliant sunlight, giving then all new hope.

'I have been thinking about the poem,' said Polka suddenly. 'I would like to see it again.' Terry duly obliged, retrieving the paper from the bag and handing it to Polka. The small boy held the verse close to his face, studying it carefully.

Crack the riddle, find the stone
Read the winning place alone
Only take a single sign
Set together in a line

Seek the Watcher, fear the foe
Burn the riddle once you know
On the journey, trust in few
Watcher watches out for you

After a while, he made a solemn announcement.

'I understand this. Now we must burn it.'

'What does it mean?' demanded Terry excitedly.

'*The winning place* means first place, explained Polka confidently. 'And *only take a single sign* means only take the first letter. Don't you see? You take the first letter from each line of the poem, and put them together in a new line. C–R–O–S–S–B–O–W. We need to find a crossbow.'

The others studied the verse and saw that Polka was correct.

'That's brilliant!' said Terry, very impressed.

'Well done, Polka,' added Gwen. 'I would never have thought of that.'

'Polka is clever at solving puzzles,' said Meeshka

proudly, 'but I am still not sure what it means.'

'Did the stranger have a crossbow, Gwen?' asked Terry.

'I have never heard that he did,' she replied, 'but we will find out. Come now, we will walk up to the village, and trust that the Bandero have not returned to the boat. I did not dare set out to look for you until I was sure they had set off back to Carthag with Hev.'

It took about an hour to walk up to Trento where the boat was moored, and the towpath had become a muddy quagmire, steaming in the warm sunshine. Whenever another boat approached they had to move off the towpath and hide in the fields that bordered the canal, just in case any Bandero were aboard. They were very tired and hungry when they finally got to the outskirts of the little village. The canal cut right through the centre of Trento, and Gwen walked on alone while the children waited out of sight. She soon returned with the good news that there was no-one around, and the boat was safely moored and unguarded. The children ran the short distance from their hiding place to the boat, and immediately went down into the hold. They were glad to settle back into the beds they had been rudely disturbed from the previous evening, and despite being very hungry, they were all soon asleep once more. It was several hours before Gwen finally wakened them, and only then because she was anxious to make a start on the journey north. It was early evening, and she had prepared a large meal. The children hadn't eaten since the previous evening and were extremely grateful to sit down to fried fish and vegetables with delicious herb bread.

After they had eaten, they ceremoniously burnt the poem riddle on the cooking stove. If they were captured and searched, no-one could find the clue now.

'Perhaps I should hide the stone somewhere?' suggested Terry.

'But what if it was found by somebody?' warned Meeshka.

'And we have six more to find,' added Polka. 'It would be best to keep them all together.'

Gwen examined Terry's waistcoat carefully. 'I will make you a secret pocket within the lining, behind the middle button,' she said. 'You can hide the black bag there, and no-one would find it without a very careful search. We will not speak of it, even amongst ourselves.'

'We will travel mostly by night,' she continued. 'That will be safer. It is important that the three of you are not all seen together, at least until we are much further north, so you must take it in turns to lead the morsk.'

'What would the Bandero do to us if they caught us?' asked Meeshka warily.

'I dare not think,' replied Gwen. 'We must make sure they never do.'

'Our father would fight them if he could get to this world!' said Polka defiantly.

'Unfortunately, the Bandero are very numerous. We must use stealth and cunning to make our way north, passing under their very noses. While you slept, I removed the plaque with the boat's name on it. Canal folk tend to remember the names of boats, and the Bandero tend to ask lots of questions. It is better to be cautious.'

'Will no-one else help us?' asked Terry.

'Perhaps,' said Gwen. 'We must wait and see. I have friends in a town well north of here, and I am hopeful. We will head for there – I can say no more at present.'

It took Gwen only a few minutes to sew the secret

pocket in Terry's waistcoat, and he was very impressed with the result. He transferred the black velvet bag and Hawk's Eye stone, and immediately felt happier that the stone was now cleverly concealed.

They set off under a sky that was on fire with the most glorious sunset Terry had ever seen. Torn and straggled clouds hovered close to the horizon, glowing orange and pink. Above these, a sapphire blue sky was dappled with countless small fleecy clouds that shimmered with every possible shade of purple. Terry had volunteered to lead the morsk first, and he patted the beast and whispered encouraging words to it as they trudged along beneath this spectacular backdrop. The gentle clomp of morsk hoof on towpath was the only sound, while the great shadow of the boat glided silently behind.

It was a very calm evening, and the stars were soon blazing forth in the darkening sky above, pulling Terry's gaze ever upward until his neck ached. He noticed several familiar constellations – The Great Bear, Cassiopeia, and The Seven Sisters were all there. Over in the east, a full Hunter's Moon rose rapidly up over the misty fields. The familiar sight was somehow comforting, as was the sweet smell of the evening dew, wafting in from the dark fields. *This is still the World*, thought Terry, *even though it is very different*. But why was it different? And why was he here? He remembered the goshawk, and how it had seemed to lure him into Crow Wood. Was that just a coincidence, or had it all been part of some devious plan to take him from his own world? Every question seemed to generate more questions. And he had no answers for any of them.

Interrogation

'The situation is very simple,' said Captain Tache bluntly, 'either you tell us where the children are, or you will live out the rest of your days in the dungeons of Castle Turuk.' Hev held the captain's steely gaze without flinching.

'Then it will have to be the dungeons,' he replied wearily, 'for I do not know where they are.'

Captain Tache had left Castle Turuk around mid-morning. The dark and threatening thunderclouds that were gathering had complimented his mood perfectly. To his surprise though, his annoyance with the Baron had eased, the further he had ridden from the isolated fortress. It had dawned on him that he was never fully comfortable within the confines of the castle keep. The stone walls, he had concluded, had a suffocating effect on him. As soon as he was away from the castle, galloping a fresh morsk along the forest trail, the rush of wind in his face had revived his spirits. Although several storms had rumbled both to the north and south of him, he had managed to stay dry on his journey back to Carthag. He had reached the city outskirts during the early evening, feeling quite upbeat. The white bases of the city's towers, dampened by the earlier rain, were glistening freshly in the late sunshine. Having no cause to hurry, he had made his way through the quiet streets towards his headquarters at a moderate pace, giving his morsk the chance to recuperate from the long gallop. Once rested and refreshed himself, and having been informed that there was a prisoner in the cells, he had decided to do the interrogation personally, and without delay.

Hev and Captain Tache were high up in one of the towers in the south-east of the city. It was situated in one of the more prosperous areas that had long been a province of the Bandero. The tower was one of four, built on the corners of a large square building. This single-storey white stone construction, typical of Carthag's tower basements, surrounded a grassy quadrangle, in the middle of which stood a white marble statue of the previous Baron. Unusually for Carthag, the towers at each corner of the complex had no linking corsas. The building served as an administration centre for two separate complements of the Bandero Guard, and several high ranking officers had billets in the upper rooms, including the captain. He had arranged for Hev to be brought up from the cells in the basement, so that he could conduct the interrogation in the comfort of his living quarters.

The room was adequately furnished, with upholstered armchairs and padded footstools, a small writing desk, and a tall pine cabinet. A lantern hung on each of the walls, giving a subdued but pleasant light. The ceiling was covered with a large tapestry, depicting some famous battle in which the Bandero had triumphed long ago, but it was in very poor condition. Captain Tache lounged comfortably in a well-worn armchair, his sturdy black leather boots propped arrogantly on a stool before him. Hev, by contrast, sat upright and rigid in his chair, directly opposite the captain.

'You would not resign yourself so willingly to the castle's dungeons if you had previous experience of them,' warned the captain.

'I do not relish the prospect, Captain,' replied Hev, 'but since I do not *know* where the children are, I cannot *tell* you where they are.'

'You say that, yet the children were seen getting onto your boat. You do not deny this.'

'I do not, Captain. We did not know then, that they were sought by the Bandero. Had we known, we would not have allowed them aboard.'

'They had been staying in your tower!'

'Apparently so – I have not long returned from Sudin, and I need to go back there directly, where I have further business to attend to. This has not yet allowed me the opportunity to visit my home tower. My wife and these three children joined me for a short while, as I collected more goods and provisions from our boathouse in the city. When the boat was stopped at the canal junction, we left the children in the hold and came to see why the boats were being searched. When we returned, the children had left. I have told your men this.'

'Why would the children run off like that?'

'I could not say, Captain. In truth, I could not really

care either. It was a relief to find them gone. I have concerns enough, simply making an honest living, without the needs of three stray children to consider.'

Captain Tache was impressed with the composure of the tall dark boater, and he didn't impress easily these days. He had many years experience of interrogation, and he had learnt how to probe a prisoner from slightly different directions during questioning.

'Where were the children going?'

'They were heading east, last time I saw them,' answered Hev truthfully.

'And their intentions?'

'Unclear. They seemed confused. They talked of wanting to go home, which I surmised to be in the deep south. My wife befriended them out of compassion, and gave them food and shelter for the night. The children knew we would be going south at the junction, and I suspect they hoped to hitch a ride with us to the ocean. Perhaps I was mistaken.'

'And where is your wife now?'

'I hope that she is tending our morsk and watching our boat. She will no doubt be anxious about my situation and hoping for my swift release. She is aware that I must return south shortly.'

'You will not be returning anywhere unless you start being more cooperative!' barked the captain, turning suddenly aggressive in an attempt to unsettle his prisoner.

Hev shrugged, but kept a wary eye on the captain. 'I can only tell you the truth,' he said blithely. Captain Tache smiled sarcastically. 'Let me know when you start,' he replied coldly. Hev gave the captain an injured look, but said no more. Tache studied his prisoner thoughtfully for a while, allowing a menacing silence to develop. Then he began his questioning again.

'Tell me about this third child – the one who came after the other two.'

'I only saw these children for a few short hours. There is little I can tell you about any of them. He was dressed differently, but in other respects he was like the first two – lost and alone.'

Hev calculated that it was better to give Captain Tache small, relatively worthless bits of information in order to keep him in as good a humour as possible. That way, he might be able to buy Gwen and the children more time to leave the district.

'What is the connection of the third child to the other two?'

'None, that I know of. The others found him by pure chance, I believe.'

'How did they travel to Carthag? And where are they coming from, these children, with their strange clothes?'

'They did not say.'

'And you did not ask? Surely you were curious?'

Hev shook his head simply. 'As I have said, I believe they probably came from the deep south, judging by their unusual clothes and speech. Perhaps they have recently escaped from some slave traders. I have not travelled beyond the southern ocean, and I am not familiar with the people of the southern empire. My concerns, Captain, lie more with my business closer to home.'

'Yet your wife seemed concerned with these children?'

'My wife arrived at the jetty, saying she had found three lost children. She asked that we give them a good meal that evening, and shelter for the night. I agreed on the condition that we sent them on their way the next day. In the event, they left of their own volition.'

Normally sombre, measured and astute, Captain Tache realised he was allowing himself to become exasperated. He couldn't quite decide whether the prisoner was keeping something back. Whatever it was, it wasn't much – he felt confident of that, but he was equally sure that his interrogation skills should have prised it out. It was particularly annoying that his men had only brought Hev in for questioning. Had he had the woman with him, he could have broken them both. A certain sergeant was about to become a corporal again for that particular lapse in duty. It was time to play his last card.

'I think perhaps my men have arrested the wrong person,' he said casually.

Hev gave him a questioning look, a sense of unease stirring in his depths.

'Yes,' continued the captain, encouraged by Hev's reaction, 'I think it would be useful to talk to your wife.'

'I can assure you that she knows no more than I,' replied Hev, doing his best to sound unconcerned.

'Well, we shall see.' Captain Tache walked over to the trapdoor and shouted down.

'Kredo! Return the prisoner to the cells. At first light, he is to be transferred to the castle, where he is to be held, pending my orders.'

'Very good, sir!' came the acknowledgement from below.

'And Kredo...'

'Sir?'

'He is to receive minimum rations for the time being.'

'Very good, sir!'

Turning back towards Hev, the captain spoke with a brusque finality. 'You have disappointed me, and it will be the worse for you because of that. We will see if a few days in the castle dungeons will loosen your tongue somewhat. In the meantime, I will determine what your wife has to say on these matters.'

'She will be able to tell you no more than I have,' replied Hev sullenly.

A spasm of anger gripped the Bandero Captain's face for an instant.

'On the contrary, I believe she will be able to tell me a great deal,' he snarled.

Hev opened his mouth to protest, but realised that this would only deepen the captain's resolve to question Gwen. Instead, he simply shrugged.

Two Bandero appeared through the trapdoor, and roughly bound Hev's hands behind his back. As a result, returning down the several storeys to the cells in the basement was an unpleasant experience for him. The guards were not overly helpful as he descended the ladders, and frequently he slipped several rungs, catching his chin on the upper rungs as he fell. By the time he reached the cells, he had many painful bruises. He expected that the journey to the castle the next day would be equally unpleasant, but he was consoled by one fact. If Tache had bought his story about the children heading south, Gwen would have a chance, at least, to get them safely north to Piree.

Hooves and Heartbeats

They had been travelling north for three days, moving mostly by night when the canal was quiet. A routine, of sorts, had been established, whereby soon after first light they would begin looking for one of the frequent jetties that were offset into the banks on either side. Some jetties could accommodate several boats together, and doubled as crossing points. Bridges were infrequent over the Carthag canals, and when they did occur, were invariably of the type that could be swung or raised clear of the water, to allow the passage of taller boats. Instead, several jetties berthed large pontoons, capable of taking several riders. These could be pulled or punted the short distance across the water. Pontoon jetties were always busier, both with canal traffic and people wishing to cross the canal. In order to avoid company, and any resulting awkward questions, Gwen always took the trouble to find a smaller jetty with just a single berth. So far at least, they had been lucky. Each morning they had found solitary moorings, some distance away from other boaters. They would tie up for the day, settling down in the hold of the boat to get what sleep they could. In the early evening they would leave the boat and find a sheltered spot, some distance from the canal and away from any prying eyes. Here they would cook their evening meal over an open fire, and enjoy some brief respite from the ever present danger of meeting the Bandero on the waterway.

The land had been gradually rising as they approached the northern limits of the Plain of Carthag, and the previous night had been a particularly tedious one. They had negotiated a long series of twelve locks, known as the Steps of Piree, and it had taken them most of the night to pass through. Frustratingly, the total distance from first lock to last was less than four miles, and normally they would have covered this distance in under an hour, but some of the locks in the Steps could take as long as half an hour to pass through, and this had delayed them considerably. Terry and Polka had been responsible for opening and closing the gates, and by the last one they were quite exhausted. They had all slept longer than usual, but when they finally emerged from the boat's hold, they were heartened by the fact that the Steps were now behind them. They found a small copse with a pleasant little stream meandering through it, just a few minutes away from the canal, and here they made their evening camp.

After their meal, they enjoyed a pleasant and comforting time, sitting together around the fire, as the autumn mists settled gently over the surrounding countryside. The smell of the wood smoke lingered in the air, rising vertically upwards, straight as an arrow. The sun had sunk gently into the west, leaving a sky ablaze with glory. Silhouetted against this fiery backdrop, a large and unwieldy V shape of wild geese lumbered slowly southwards, seeking warmer climes for the oncoming winter. Terry noted their passing, and knew also what it meant.

Although it was time to return to the boat, each of them felt reluctant to break the tranquillity of the moment. Polka had been watching Gwen across the campfire for several minutes, when he suddenly posed an abrupt question.

'Why don't you and Hev have any children?'

'Polka!' admonished Meeshka immediately, 'that is not a polite question.'

Gwen smiled at them both to show that she had not been offended.

'Because, Master Polka, the time is not yet right,' she replied. 'Hev has worked hard on the canals for several years. We own our boat now, and we work for nobody but ourselves. I have a market stall, and we have managed to save some money. One day soon we plan to move south, and then perhaps it will be the right time to think of a family.'

'And because of us, that day is now further away,' said Meeshka miserably.

Gwen reached out and squeezed her hand. 'You must not talk that way. None of us know how this will turn out in the end. Even if we had known Hev would be arrested by the Bandero, we would not have abandoned you. I have been thinking about this – Hev will try to buy us enough time to reach Piree. I do not know precisely what he will say, but he will try to mislead them. He cannot tell them where we are, because he does not know exactly where we are, and it is safer that way. Once the Bandero realise this, he will likely be released. Baron Hart can be cruel, but he is not needlessly so. In the meantime, we must continue our journey north.'

Some small bats flickered over their heads, fading rapidly into the twilight gloom away from the fire. Terry watched them for a while, and then a question occurred to him. 'Gwen, what will happen when we get to Piree? Does the canal continue all the way to this ravine place?'

'No, Piree is the northernmost town for boat trade. The canal goes no further. All being well, we should reach there tonight. Then we must leave the boat and go north by morsk.'

'Where will we get morsk?' asked Meeshka.

'You will recall I spoke of some friends before? Hev and I have known the people who own one of the taverns in Piree for many years. They will be able to get us four travelling morsk. This towbeast that pulls the boat is a good animal, but it was not bred to run. Our friends will take care of it while we are gone. I am hopeful that because the three of you are light, we can pack enough provisions on the morsk and still make good time. The summer is drawing to a close, and we must not get trapped in the mountains when the snows come.'

'I saw some snow geese heading south,' said Terry. Gwen nodded significantly and cast a thoughtful glance at the darkened sky. 'Winter comes early to the Whitelands,' she said gravely.

'But where will we get provisions?' persisted Meeshka gloomily.

'You worry too much, my pretty one,' laughed Gwen. 'The boat is well stocked – enough to last us a month at least.'

'But if we have to find seven stones it may take much longer than a month,' said Polka, catching something of Meeshka's sombre mood.

'It may do, or we may find all seven by tomorrow. Listen to me, children – we cannot be certain where this journey will take us, but none of us will be free from its burden until it is over. We must travel with hope and trust, not fear and despair. I believe that we will succeed in this quest, and you must too.'

There was a short silence while they each contemplated this advice.

'I think Gwen is right,' said Terry at last. 'I have no idea what we are doing here, but I have a strong feeling that.., well, it's hard to explain.'

Meeshka looked at Terry with interest. 'What do you feel?' she asked earnestly.

'Well, I think that in some way, this was planned – *we are meant to find the stones.*'

'Who would plan such a thing?'

'I don't know. Perhaps this stranger that Hev and Mozz have talked about.'

'But why would the stranger hide the seven stones just so we might find them?'

'I don't know that either,' admitted Terry, shaking his head. 'It doesn't make sense, but there must be something we haven't understood yet.'

'No doubt that is true,' agreed Gwen, 'and perhaps

there are some things we will never understand. But we must try our best anyway. We should take one step at a time. For now, it is enough for us to know that we must find the Watcher. As to what happens after that, we shall just have to wait and see.'

Meeshka smiled. 'You are right of course,' she sighed, 'and that is just what our parents would have told us. I think perhaps I am just feeling a little homesick.'

'Well,' said Gwen cheerfully, 'when we get to Piree you will have a proper bed once more, instead of dusty mattresses to sleep on. And the very best Tavern food that Piree has to offer! Come now, it is time to leave.'

They returned to the boat, but they waited until it was completely dark and the other canal users were moored up for the night, before they quietly slipped their mooring and set off. Their usual routine was for Terry and Polka to lead the morsk until about midnight, when they would stop for a hot drink and biscuits. Then Gwen and Meeshka would take over on the towpath while the boys went on the upper deck and tended the rudder.

After the boys had been trudging along the towpath for about three hours, they began to get weary. Polka had been pressing Terry for more information about his world, but Terry found himself strangely reluctant to give the details the younger boy sought. He could not fully justify to himself why this was so, but that simply added to his irritation. Polka, for his part, was frustrated by Terry's reticence to properly explain what such things as T.V. and Internet and mobiles were. As a result, they had lapsed into a somewhat hostile silence.

The moon, now waning, had risen behind a bank of clouds in the east. Its face was hidden, but it cast an orange glow down beneath the cloud-base. It looked as if some great chasm had opened up in the Earth's surface, and the light from some secret underworld was leaking up to the surface. At any other time, Terry would have thought it a wondrous sight, but tonight he was tired and annoyed by Polka's constant questioning.

All of a sudden, Polka crouched down and placed his palm on the ground.

'Some riders are coming,' he said, turning and peering into the total blackness behind them. Terry turned and listened carefully, but could hear nothing.

'Are you sure?' he asked.

Polka didn't waste time replying, but instead ran back to the boat.

'Gwen! Gwen! Quickly! Some riders are coming! Four or five!'

Gwen came running down onto the deck.

'Listen carefully,' she said urgently. 'Unhitch the morsk and take it well off into the fields. We will steer the boat over to the far bank and moor it. Stay hidden until they are well past. Quickly now!'

Terry could hear the distant thunder of hooves himself now, approaching fast. Frantically he struggled with the tether knot on the morsk's neck harness. Normally he would have had it undone in seconds, but for once it seemed unusually tight.

'Quickly!' urged Polka.

'I'm trying!'

The boat's momentum had carried it slightly forward of the boys and the morsk, putting a tension in the rope and making things even more difficult for Terry. Gwen could not swing the rudder and coast to the opposite bank until the tether was undone, so all eyes were set anxiously on Terry.

'There!' he yelled at last. Grabbing the halter of the surprised morsk, he yanked it off the towpath and into the dark fields, with Polka by his side.

'Meeshka! Pull the rope up!' shouted Gwen from back up on the bridge. The riders were only three hundred metres off now. Gwen did not dare steer too sharply into the far bank for fear that the stern of the boat would swing out into the middle of the canal. Carefully she grazed the western bank with the port side and let the friction bring the boat to a halt. Had the moon not been behind a cloud, the riders must surely have seen Meeshka on deck. As it was though, she had the rope pulled up just in time, and jumped down into the hold as the morskmen appeared out of the blackness.

There were four of them, their characteristic Bandero capes trailing behind them in the slipstream. The tow path was not wide enough for them to ride abreast, so they rode single file but bunched close together. Meeshka peeped cautiously out of the hold as they went past. She was just breathing a sigh of relief when the last of the riders suddenly pulled back on the antlers of his morsk and brought it to a shuddering halt. The other three riders had not realised he had stopped and disappeared onwards into the darkness. The man remained astride his morsk, the beast's breath steaming out into the cool night air in great misty pants. He was an accomplished rider, and manoeuvred his animal expertly in the tight space, turning it around and holding it steady while studying the boat. He wore the round peaked cap of a Bandero captain, and the buckles on his knee-length boots shone dimly in the moonlight.

Meeshka hardly dared draw breath – her heart was beating so loudly she was sure she would be heard.

It was unusual for a boat not to be moored in one of the jetties at night, and clearly the rider was troubled by this. It was also unusual for the morsk not to be tethered close by. The rider peered into the blackness on the far side of the boat, seeking the familiar silhouette of a towbeast. Meeshka dared not raise her head out of the hold to see what was happening, but she could feel the dilemma of the rider. He trotted his morsk back and forth, the length of the boat, whilst trying to decide what to do. Had the boat been on the near bank he would certainly have come aboard to investigate further. As it was, he hesitated for a while, debating whether to try and rouse the occupants of the boat. Then he turned to look up the towpath, and seemed to reach a decision. His colleagues had clearly remained unaware that he had stopped, for they were now not even in earshot. Suddenly the rider kicked his heels into the flanks of his morsk, and urged it back into a gallop, chasing after the others as if his life depended on it.

It was fully five minutes before Gwen and Meeshka dared venture onto the deck, and a further five before Terry and Polka emerged from the darkness on the other side, whispering cautiously. It took several attempts to throw the rope over to the boys, but scrabbling amongst the shallows Terry was able to retrieve it and hitch up the morsk once more. Then they pulled the boat over and moored up again on the eastern bank.

'They were Bandero,' said Meeshka, confirming everyone's fears, 'and they were looking for us. I just know it.'

'We can't be certain of that,' cautioned Gwen, 'but I

think we must assume you are right. This complicates matters.'

'How far are we from Piree?' asked Terry.

'About an hour,' she answered.

'We should go back,' urged Meeshka anxiously.

They considered this suggestion in grim silence for a while. 'No,' said Terry quietly. 'We must press on immediately.'

'But why?' asked Meeshka, close to tears. 'If they have gone to Piree, we should not go anywhere near there.'

Terry shook his head patiently. 'If they have ridden from Carthag, they have been travelling for four or five hours. They will be at Piree in just a few minutes at that pace, and they will need to rest for the night. That is our opportunity. We must get there, hide the boat, and get out of Piree again before they start their search for us.' Terry could feel a change coming over himself – a sense of responsibility for placing his new friends in the danger they now found themselves in. Even so, he was surprised to hear himself talk with such calm assurance. He looked questioningly at Gwen. 'Do you think your friends would mind being disturbed in the middle of the night?'

'I am sure they would not,' replied Gwen enthusiastically. 'That is a splendid plan, Terry, and there is no time to lose. For tonight, we must forego our cup of nettle tea and biscuits. You boys must take a second shift with the morsk – Meeshka and I must pack provisions for the journey further north.' Meeshka nodded compliantly, but the anxious look in her eyes remained.

Terry and Polka returned to the towpath without grumbling, their previous differences forgotten. They roused the morsk with some difficulty. It had settled down for the night, still in its neck harness, and was reluctant to take up the strain once more. Only by both of them tugging hard on its antlers did they manage to coax it back into motion. Once settled back into the routine though, it continued steadily forward into the night. Polka then climbed up on its back, and draping his arms around its neck, he promptly went to sleep. *He is only eight*, thought Terry sympathetically. And for the first time, Terry began to understand that growing up was not about getting older. It was about having responsibilities.

The Enemy in Waiting

'Next time your captain pulls up at full gallop, I suggest you make it your business to notice,' barked Captain Tache irritably. His three companions stared sheepishly at their feet.

'My apologies, Captain,' replied Corporal Grej. 'The waning moon was still low, and the sound of four morsk on the hard towpath was considerable, as you know.'

'My point was, Corporal Grej, that there was only the sound of *three* morsk!'

'Quite so, Captain,' said the junior officer, realising from his captain's tone that future debate on the issue would be dangerous.

They had pulled up outside a tavern in Piree, and dismounted at the rear of the building, next to the stable block. Corporal Grej and the two ratings lingered in the shadows whilst Captain Tache surveyed the hostelry. The Anchor Tavern was one of the larger taverns in Piree, and occupied a prominent position in the centre of town, close to the canal moorings. During high summer, it would still have been full to the brim with light and life, even at this late hour. Now though, with the season over, it stood in sombre darkness, but for the flicker of a candle in one of the upper rooms.

'See to the morsk,' said Captain Tache in a more measured tone. 'I will advise the owner that he is still open.'

Ten minutes later, after a short conversation between the owner and Captain Tache, they were ushered into the saloon bar. They had the whole room to themselves, and the captain had made it clear that this was to remain the case for the remainder of their visit. He kicked his riding boots off and sank wearily into a chair, putting his feet up on one of the small tables. There were rather too many tables and chairs scattered around the room, making it feel quite cluttered. In addition, the ceiling rafters were too low for a man of reasonable height, lending the room a cramped and claustrophobic atmosphere. There was, however, a large fireplace on the wall opposite the bar, which gave a sense of cosiness amongst the jumble of furniture. A large fire had been roaring earlier, and the charcoal embers still glowed contentedly.

'We have lost two days on the south and east canals,' growled Tache angrily. 'The prisoner back in Turuk will regret suggesting that the children might be found there. I begin to suspect he knew all along that their intention was to head north.'

'Perhaps they have met up with the woman once more,' ventured Corporal Grej cautiously.

'Whether or not the children are with her,' replied Tache, 'the woman herself must surely be in Piree by now. Your failure to get a single confirmed sighting of her since Carthag is a particular irritation to me!'

'It is a concern, Captain,' nodded Grej earnestly, 'but these boat people are notorious for sticking together. Always, they say they have seen nothing. There simply hasn't been time for a more thorough interrogation.'

Tache grunted unsympathetically. 'The woman should never have been released in the first place,' he muttered angrily, and then lapsed into a smouldering silence, his dark eyes fixated on the embers of the fire.

In the background, the tavern owner glided unobtrusively into the room. Having observed the tense silence for a few moments, he politely cleared his throat.

'What is it?' snarled Captain Tache.

'Begging your pardon, sir, I have prepared two rooms as you requested. Will there be anything else?'

'Yes, there will. We have just ridden for over four hours without decent rest or refreshment. You will prepare a meal for us, and be quick about it. There is to be no ale mind – we shall rise at first light.'

'Very good, sir.'

Tache caught the look of dismay in the eyes of the other Bandero. First light, he realised, would only be four hours away. He remembered his own contempt for Baron Hart when the latter had given him little rest before returning from Castle Turuk to Carthag.

'At least,' he added more soberly, 'I myself will rise at first light. I have reason to apprehend somebody.'

The tavern owner, whose name was Herstan, merely inclined his head courteously.

'A boating woman,' continued Captain Tache, watching Herstan closely, 'called Gwen – the wife of a trader known as Hev.'

Herstan nodded noncommittally.

'Do you know of these people?'

'No, sir, I do not recall the names.'

'A youngish woman, who has arrived in Piree just recently? Perhaps in the company of children?'

'I have not seen or heard of such a woman, sir, but I can make enquiries for you if you so desire.'

'Yes, I do so desire, but see that it is done..., discreetly. You may go now, and do not be long with the food.'

'My pleasure, sir.' Herstan slid silently from the room in a practised manner.

The three other Bandero removed their capes and made themselves comfortable by the fireplace, enjoying the remnants of its warmth.

'The woman must be here by now,' muttered Tache, almost to himself.

'We will find her, sir,' assured Corporal Grej. 'If you rise at first light, then so do we.' Captain Tache was gratified by the loyalty of his corporal, and inwardly congratulated himself on his leadership skills in comparison with the Baron.

'Join me when you are rested, Grej. If she is here, she is receiving food and shelter from somebody. I will check out the main moorings at dawn, but of course it is possible she came by morsk. Mingle with the locals and see what you can find out. There is always the chance she went south, and we missed her. Or she may have avoided the canals altogether, and struck out across the plain. Then again, her husband indicated he did not expect she would leave

Carthag, and she may still be in hiding there. What we need is a single sighting – she cannot simply have disappeared. For all our sakes I hope she is here in Piree, and the children too. The Baron will be growing impatient.'

'What is the importance of these children, sir?' asked Bruno, one of the unranked men.

'A good soldier simply follows his orders,' replied Tache curtly, 'but you can be sure that both I and the Baron will look favourably on the man who finds them.'

'People say they have magical stones of power,' persisted Bruno unwisely.

'People say many things, but I say this – busy yourself with the task in hand, and not the idle gossip of the common people! I will tolerate no less!'

'Yes, sir!'

The soldiers lapsed into an uncomfortable silence once more until Herstan returned with bowls of steaming stew, and fresh bread from the evening bake. He hovered politely in the background while the men ate, busying himself with unnecessary tidying. Towards the end of the meal, there was a knocking sound at the rear door of the tavern.

Corporal Grej and the two soldiers continued greedily mopping the last of their stew with chunks of bread, but Captain Tache immediately stopped eating and stared hard at Herstan.

'A little late to be receiving guests, is it not?'

'Yes indeed, Captain,' commented Herstan calmly, 'perhaps your entire company will favour my humble tavern tonight.'

'I entirely doubt that. Perhaps you had better see who calls at this hour.'

Herstan inclined his head graciously, and maintaining a

calm and unhurried demeanour, he left the room and walked steadily down the short hallway that led to the back door. He felt the presence of the Bandero Captain behind him, even before he spoke.

'Perhaps I should also see who calls at this late hour,' declared Captain Tache, calmly drawing the long dagger that all Bandero officers carried. As he did so, the person on the other side of the door knocked again, with greater urgency.

Puree

About five-hundred metres from the outskirts of the town, Gwen and the children came to the final lock on the North Canal. Normally, a lock-keeper would oversee the passage of all vessels through this important gateway – at this hour though, he had long since retired for the night. His small octagonal cottage, built by the side of the lock, stood dark and silent in the cool night air – not even a candle flickered from any of the high arched windows. Wearily, Terry and Polka turned the creaking sluice handles on the upper gates, then sat astride the black and white balanced beams as the boat rose slowly up from the dark depths of the lock well. Perhaps it was because they were so tired, but it seemed to take forever before the water was level with the upper pound. Eventually, Terry was able to swing the big gates open, while Polka re-hitched the morsk and pulled the boat clear of the lock. They had arrived in Piree.

They went only another fifty metres or so before mooring up once again, but not in a recognised jetty. Gwen did not want to go any further into the town without checking it was safe to do so. As the boat swished into the tall reeds that grew in the shallows, they disturbed the night roost of two waterfowl. The birds scurried over the water with a loud squawk but did not take to the air, disappearing quickly into the cover of the far bank. Gwen jumped lightly from the boat and onto the towpath. She did not unhitch the morsk, but shortened the tether considerably so it could not stray far from the boat. It seemed to appreciate that its work was done for the time being, and sank gratefully to its knees in the long grass that grew by the side of the towpath.

'I must leave you for a while,' said Gwen. 'I will walk into the town and wake my good friends Herstan and Freda. We must be sure it is safe to enter the town. If all goes well, I will return within the hour and we will take the boat into Piree and conceal it. I don't expect another boat will come by tonight, but if one should, stay inside. They will not be very happy about it, but they will punt around you to get past. I want you all to stay hidden in the hold until I return.'

'Be careful,' pleaded Meeshka.

'Don't worry, my pretty one,' smiled Gwen. 'I will be back soon.'

The children watched Gwen disappear up the towpath and into the darkness. They suddenly felt very alone. 'Come on,' said Terry grimly. 'There's nothing we can do but wait.' The three of them climbed into the hold of the boat and locked the hatch from inside.

The town of Piree was built around a large rectangular jetty that brought the north canal to a sudden halt, like the bar on a letter T. Leading off this giant jetty were numerous short moorings, both north and south, that more often than not were enclosed by wooden shanties to make a float-in boathouse. On the eastern bar, there were several dry-dock facilities, and this was the industrial heart of the town. Most of the boats that travelled the four canals out of Carthag had been built in Piree, and most of the residents of Piree had something to do with boats, in one way or another.

Gwen hurried down the towpath towards the black silhouette of the town centre. Buildings began to loom up on either side of the canal – tall crooked shadows, standing apparently lifeless in the dead of the night. In reality, she knew that any one of them might harbour the four Bandero who had passed them an hour earlier. Occasionally, she passed some drunk or down-and-out, propping themselves up against a wall or staggering erratically homewards. Mostly though, the streets were deserted.

The odd building had a lantern still burning, and she had no difficulty finding her way to the Anchor Tavern, close to the central jetties. She decided to go to the back door, just in case any guests were still in the bar. At this time of year she expected that the tavern would be closed up by now, and Herstan and Freda would be in their bed. Nevertheless, she was reluctant to take any chances, given that the Bandero were in town. She stood in the deepest shadows by the back door for several minutes, listening for any signs of life within the tavern. There was no sound, and her confidence grew. The stable block to her left was also quiet – she briefly considered checking it first, but decided not to in case she disturbed some stable lad. The fewer people who knew she was there, the better.

In Carthag, the Bandero had their own commandeered properties, and staff to attend to their every need. Gwen fully expected it would be the same here in Piree, so there was little risk that they would have come to the Anchor Tavern at this late hour. Eventually, she plucked up her courage and knocked. She knew she would have to wait a while before Herstan raised himself from his bed, but she felt vulnerable standing there alone, and after half a minute she knocked again with greater urgency.

At that point things began to happen very quickly. She heard the door being unbolted from inside, but at the same moment, a miniature tornado seemed to rush in from her left, hurling her into the dark corner of the small courtyard that enclosed the rear entrance. She lost her balance and fell heavily to the ground, lying face down on the cold cobble stones, winded and temporarily stunned. She turned her head painfully, and looked up to see the tavern door open. The light from inside flooded out, followed very soon afterwards by a Bandero captain with dagger drawn.

Standing before Captain Tache was a child of perhaps thirteen years old. A ragamuffin girl, of scrawny appearance. Her brown hair fell in a tangled mess of curls onto her slender shoulders, and she wore a grubby brown dress with short sleeves. She stood, barefooted and hands on hips, staring impudently up at the Bandero captain.

'I want to speak to Herstan,' she demanded rudely.

Herstan eased past Captain Tache and held up the lantern. 'Clumber!' he said. 'What are you doing here at this time of night?'

'I got sent by me Gran to tell yer,' replied Clumber excitedly.

'To tell me what, child?'

'Me mother's bad with the fever, see. Go fetch yer Uncle Herstan, says me Gran. Tell 'im he's to come o'er here right now.'

'Who is this child, Barman?' asked Captain Tache hotly. He felt his dignity had been affronted by the situation, and he re-sheathed his dagger with obvious irritation.

'This is my niece, Captain.'

Captain Tache would have liked to make a cutting reply but none came readily to mind. 'Well, you had better deal with the situation,' he said lamely.

'Thank you, sir. If you and your men wouldn't mind showing yourselves to your rooms, I must wake my wife and let her know that I am going out. Clumber, please follow me.'

'No, Herstan, I got to get straight back. Me gran said I must.'

'Very well then. Tell your grandmother that I will be over directly.'

Clumber nodded and waited for the two men to return back into the tavern. She made as if to go, but cut back once she heard the bolt of the door slide across. She found Gwen still lying where she had fallen in the shadows, and helped her to her feet.

'Sshh!' cautioned Clumber. 'Don't say owt 'til we get round the other side.'

Gwen was shocked at how close she had come to presenting herself to the Bandero Captain, and was content, for the time being at least, to trust the strange skinny girl who had just saved her from arrest.

'Sorry I had to push yer, but I had to stop yer somehow.'

'But, I don't understand…who are you?' asked Gwen.

'I'm Clumber! Don't worry, we know who you are. Are the strangers still on your boat?'

Gwen was stunned by the question, and did not know how to reply, so she said nothing, merely staring down at Clumber uncertainly. The skinny girl pulled her to a stop by her arm, and grinned up at her.

'I know 'bout the other kids – we all do. We know 'bout the Bandero having got Hev too, but don't worry, we'll soon 'ave 'im rescued.'

Gwen gasped with surprise. For several moments all she could do was gape at Clumber, her mouth open in astonishment. So many questions came to her mind at once that she didn't know which one to ask.

'Are we going to your mother's?' she tried.

'Not exactly,' replied Clumber happily.

'But shouldn't we get back to help your gran?'

Clumber stopped again and looked up at Gwen in obvious amusement.

'I'm an orphan – I never knew me mother, or me gran, come to that.'

'But you told your Uncle Herstan that…'

'Herstan ain't me uncle,' laughed Clumber. 'Him an' Freda have jus' been lookin' after me for a bit.'

'But…'

'Look, just wait 'til we get inside an' it'll make a good deal more sense.'

They had been walking away from the tavern by a side street, but had twice taken left turns, and Gwen felt they must be coming back towards the building from a different direction. Instead, she found they had turned into a blind alley, blocked at its end by a windowless gable wall of imposing stone. At the base of the wall, an untidy pile of rotten wood and broken barrels had collected.

'What are we doing here?' she asked, perplexed. Clumber did not reply, but busied herself with removing some of the wood and barrels that had been strategically placed to conceal a small iron grate, built into the base of the wall. She then knelt down and gripped this firmly, lifting it up, and at the same time twisting it forwards. Although the grate looked securely mounted and impossible to shift, with a sudden click it came away in Clumber's arms.

'Crawl in,' she commanded confidently. Gwen sank to her knees and crawled through the opening into pitch blackness. Clumber followed, dragging items from the woodpile after her in order to hide the grate once more. She then re-attached the grate with practised ease. After it clicked back into place, she shook it vigorously to test it was firmly fastened in place. When satisfied, she crawled past Gwen in the darkness.

'C'mon,' she whispered happily. They crawled down a narrow tunnel for about three metres, which ended abruptly with some sort of wooden barrier. Clumber searched deftly for a hidden catch, which when she released it, allowed the wooden panel to be slid sideways. Some light now leaked into their tunnel, and Gwen could see that there was a further wooden barrier immediately in front of them. Clumber simply pushed on this, and two small doors swung outwards into what looked like a small storeroom. As they climbed through into the room, Gwen realised they were emerging from a small cupboard, standing against the back wall of the storeroom. Within the room were several barrels, stacked neatly against one wall, and a line of shelving filled with demijohns and other sundry items.

'Where are we?' she whispered anxiously.

'You'll see,' replied Clumber with evident enjoyment. The dim light in the small room came from light leaking around and under the door in the opposite wall. This clearly led to a well-lit room on the far side. Clumber hurried over to this door and knocked boldly three times.

'It's me!' she shouted through to the other side. After a short pause, a bolt was withdrawn and the door opened. Bright light flooded through to the storeroom, causing Gwen to shield her eyes with one hand. Clumber led her into the room by her other hand.

'Look who I've brought!' announced Clumber proudly, clearly feeling very pleased with herself.

Gwen found herself in a long, narrow room with a low roof. In the centre of the left hand wall, part of the stonework had been removed to form a fireplace and chimney, and a copper kettle swung over some glowing amber coals. A large oak table in front of the fire formed the focal point of the room, and several upturned barrels around it made makeshift chairs. At the table, with the remnants of a meal still between them, sat two men who Gwen did not know. Standing to one side was a short, dark haired woman who had opened the door.

'Freda!' cried Gwen in delight, as she recognised her friend.

'Welcome to our little secret society,' smiled Freda, hugging Gwen warmly. 'You must be tired and full of questions. I'm afraid we can't offer you proper refreshments with the Bandero around upstairs, but Clumber will make you a hot drink.'

'Where are we?' asked Gwen.

'In the ale-cask cellar, directly underneath the Anchor Tavern,' replied Freda smiling. 'You came in by the emergency exit!'

Gwen nodded in astonishment. 'I've been in the tavern many times, but I never even knew this room existed.'

'It's only recently that we've cleared it out, and brightened it up a bit,' explained Freda. 'We needed a headquarters that the Bandero could not barge their way into.' Gwen looked over at the two men, who were both staring at her.

'This is Calvos and Dreyfus,' said Freda. 'They are friends and comrades.'

The men stood up and shook hands with Gwen. Both were about thirty. Calvos was the taller, and had long, dark hair, tied back in a pony tail. Dreyfus had a tanned complexion, and curly dark brown hair with a moustache.

'I think I have seen you on the canals before,' said Gwen to Dreyfus.

'Most likely,' he replied. 'I have worked the canals for some time, and know your husband well.'

'You know Hev?'

'We have often drunk together when trading with the southern merchants.'

'And you know he has been arrested by the Bandero?'

'I do. That is one of the reasons we are here tonight.'

Freda manoeuvred two upturned barrels into comfortable positions by the table.

'Come and sit down a moment,' she said. 'There is a lot to explain.'

The four of them sat around the table, and Gwen waited for somebody to speak.

Calvos, who had said nothing up to that point, suddenly caught Gwen's eye and smiled. 'There are not many of us,' he began, 'the people you see here, and Herstan, and two or three more. These two secret rooms under the tavern have recently become our headquarters. For some time now, we have been researching the legend of the stranger and the stone – some say more than one stone – and gathering testimony from those who met him. One even names him as Yalyf, although that name is not widely known. From all that we have gathered, one thing remained clear – strange travellers would one day return, and they would be children. We have been expecting them, and planning how to help them when the time came. When first we received word that two strange children were staying in your tower, we have been watching you. As you came north from Carthag with the children, you were discreetly followed.'

'You were not so alone as you thought during your evening camps,' added Dreyfus with a broad grin.

'Herstan and Freda thought you would most likely come to them when you arrived in Piree,' continued Calvos. 'When the Bandero came to the tavern tonight, Clumber was sent to keep watch for you.' Clumber had placed a mug of steaming tea before Gwen, and couldn't restrain herself from laughing out loud.

'Aye, an' I only just managed to stop her walking right in on them!'

As Clumber spoke, somebody knocked lightly on the heavy door that led out of the cellar and up into the tavern. Everybody in the room froze, listening intently. The knock had been an unusual rhythm, three raps, then two, then one. It repeated, a little louder.

'It is Herstan,' said Freda confidently, moving quickly over to the doorway.

Calvos nodded to Freda, who then withdrew a large bolt on the inside of the door. Herstan strode briskly into the room, holding a lantern.

'All is well,' he said calmly. 'The Bandero have settled for the night – they believe I have gone to my mother's.' He then turned to Gwen with a warm smile.

'It is good to see you, Gwen,' he said.

'And you too, although not in the circumstances I had imagined.'

'Yes, the Bandero guests were an unpleasant surprise. However, for now they are sleeping soundly, but they will rise at dawn.' Calvos and Dreyfus exchanged glances.

'Well then, there is little time to spare,' continued Calvos. We must hide the boat at once, and get the children to safety.'

'Yes,' agreed Gwen anxiously. 'I have left the children alone on the boat. I must return at once.'

'What was your purpose in travelling north?' asked Calvos

'We need to go to the mountains. There is a place called the Ravine of Silence.'

'You seek the Watcher?'

'Yes. Terry, one of the children, arrived with a verse that seemed to suggest this. Then later, by the canal, he was given a message by someone who claims to have met the stranger many years ago. Terry was told to seek someone who knew he was coming.'

'Who gave this message?'

'A man called Mozz. He has done some work for Hev before. I do not know him well.'

'Is he trustworthy?'

'I cannot say for certain, but he did not betray us to the Bandero when they searched the boats outside Carthag.'

'At least then, he is not a Bandero spy, but the Emperor has many eyes and ears up here too. I would like to know more about this man's dealings with the stranger.'

'He spoke only to the eldest boy. I have not seen him since.'

Dreyfus rose from the table and gathered his cape around him.

'I think I know this man Mozz,' he said thoughtfully. 'If it is the person I think it is, he keeps himself to himself, but I have heard no ill word against him.'

Calvos nodded. 'We will make enquiries later. For now, you know what must be done?'

'Yes,' replied Dreyfus knowingly. 'I will open up one of the covered dockyards. The Bandero will look first for the boat on the wharf. Then they will search the boathouses. They will check the dockyards last, if at all.' He turned to Gwen with a smile. 'By the time they do, your boat will have a fresh coat of paint.'

'We can't fetch the children here,' said Freda anxiously, 'it's too dangerous.'

'If the road leads north, I see no cause for delay,' replied Calvos. 'Gwen, do you think you could ride north at dawn, assuming we can get four morsk?'

'Yes, oh yes! That is what we had hoped for. We had seen the Bandero ride ahead of us, and planned to be gone before they rose. We have provisions packed ready on the boat.'

'You will need more,' said Freda firmly, 'and tents, and other camping equipment. I can get them.'

'Very well,' agreed Calvos, 'we will rendezvous later in the dockyard.'

'I should go with them,' announced Clumber suddenly.

'What is this?' asked Herstan sternly.

'I can be useful. I've proved that tonight. Lemme go with Gwen and the strangers. They don't know the way, anyhows.'

'Do *you*?' asked Calvos suspiciously.

'Yes!' said Clumber urgently. 'I've been up near the ravine when the slave traders 'ad me. Before Herstan an' Freda helped me.'

Calvos looked across at Freda and Herstan for an answer.

'She is still so young,' said Freda uncertainly.

'So are the strangers,' countered Clumber obstinately.

'Herstan?' asked Calvos grimly.

Herstan paused thoughtfully before replying. 'She is versatile,' he sighed at last. 'She will be no extra burden, and possibly very useful.'

'Thanks, Herstan!' cried Clumber jubilantly.

'Quickly then,' said Calvos. 'We need five morsk, and we must move without delay. The dawn is less than two hours away.'

'I can arrange the morsk,' said Herstan confidently.

'And I will see to it that they are loaded with everything you will need,' added Freda.

'So then,' concluded Calvos, 'I will return to the boat with Gwen. Clumber, you will accompany us. Dreyfus will prepare the dockyard.' They all rose, but as they started to leave, Gwen remembered something.

'Wait,' she said. 'Clumber said something about rescuing Hev.' Calvos frowned sternly. 'Did she indeed?' Clumber moved towards the door, avoiding his eye.

'That is partly our fault Calvos,' said Herstan apologetically. 'We have talked too freely in front of the girl. Hev and Gwen are trusted friends, and our greatest concern is their safety.' Calvos nodded and turned seriously to Gwen. 'Clumber has spoken rashly. We had discussed a rescue attempt, but the latest word from Carthag is that Hev has already been removed to Castle Turuk. There is little we can do to help him now – I am sorry.'

'I understand,' said Gwen softly, tears welling in her eyes. 'We must trust to the benevolence of the Baron now.' Calvos nodded gently, his brown eyes showing he understood. 'Come now,' he said. 'There is much to do before dawn.'

Gwen, Calvos, and Clumber left the tavern by the back entrance once more, and moved silently through the empty streets, encountering no-one. Once on the towpath, they abandoned caution and ran through the night, until the boat loomed up out of the darkness, moored just where Gwen had left it. All was silent. She clambered breathlessly aboard and knocked lightly on the hold hatch. To her considerable relief, she heard it being unbolted from below, and Terry's sleepy head emerged into the cool night air. The three of them were safe and sound, having been undisturbed while they waited for Gwen to return. They were hurriedly introduced to Calvos and Clumber, and the plan was explained to them. Then Calvos took the morsk and led the boat into the centre of Piree, glancing anxiously to the east for any sign of the coming dawn.

Gwen and the children gathered together the spare clothes and provisions they had already laid out, sorting everything into manageable packs, whilst Clumber gazed on in rapturous curiosity. She could not take her eyes off Meeshka and Polka in particular, until Gwen gently reminded her it was rude to stare.

'Sorry, but I can't believe it's really the strangers,' she said earnestly. Meeshka smiled cautiously at her, and Clumber's happiness was complete.

Once in the heart of the town, a clever system of wide, raised walkways allowed the morsk to continue towing through the crowded boat lanes and past the cluttered jetties. By the time they reached the covered dockyard on the eastern bar, Dreyfus was ready and waiting for them. There were two mooring bays inside, one of which was a sealed dry-dock and held the skeleton hull of a vessel under construction. The other was empty, and open to the waterway. The boat glided smoothly into it.

'Calvos and I will have a new coat of paint on this by the time the Bandero get down here,' said Dreyfus confidently. 'The red boat they are looking for will be a green one!'

'Remember it needs a new name too,' said Polka eagerly.

'True enough,' agreed Dreyfus. 'What would you have me name it Gwen?'

Gwen paused, thinking carefully for a moment. 'Name it 'Hope',' she said at last.

Meeshka caught her eye and smiled. 'Good choice,' she said contentedly.

Herstan arrived shortly afterwards leading two morsk, their saddlebags loaded with camping equipment.

'Freda has put some warmer clothes and sturdy footwear in,' he explained. 'It will be much colder further north.'

'Thank you,' said Gwen gratefully, 'they will be much appreciated.'

'Clumber come with me,' continued Herstan, 'we have another three morsk to fetch. Make haste, the dawn is here.'

Terry studied the new morsk carefully. He could see that these creatures were a different breed to the tow morsk, which now stood morosely in a corner of the yard. They were taller, to start with, and both athletic and highly strung. Their eyes roamed wildly, and they swished their tails impatiently. Terry raised his hand to stroke one but it jerked its head away temperamentally. Polka, who did not even come up to the height of the saddle, looked on warily with a pensive expression.

Herstan and Clumber returned quite quickly with another three animals, and these were soon loaded with the provisions from the boat.

'So then,' said Calvos when they were ready, 'you young strangers must quickly become expert morsk riders.' Terry, Meeshka and Polka were helped up into their saddles and the rudiments of riding were quickly explained. There were no reins as such, the rider held a special grip on the raised pommel at the front of the saddle. There were also leather fenders and stirrup irons, which Terry was vaguely familiar with, having once done some horse-riding. There was a leather halter around the neck, the end of which could be held in the hands as they gripped the pommel.

'Tug the halter to stop,' explained Calvos, 'and kick in on one side to turn. For sharp turns and emergency stops, they will respond if you grasp an antler.'

Herstan had chosen a particularly small and good natured morsk for Polka, but even so he could see the boy was nervous.

'You will soon get used to it,' said Herstan gently.

'We have ridden a similar beast called a pony,' explained Meeshka, 'but Polka has not had much experience yet.' Clumber had leapt upon her morsk in an expert fashion and was strutting up and down on it, desperate to show off.

'Clumber, I will reconsider the decision to allow you to go if you do not behave yourself,' said Herstan sternly. Clumber glowered sulkily at him, but said nothing and dismounted to wait patiently.

'Thank you for all you have done my friend,' said Gwen to Herstan, 'and thank you also Calvos, Dreyfus. We are all in your debt.' Calvos nodded seriously. 'I do not know what you will find in the north, or what this Watcher will tell you, but I believe that the happiness of all our people is tied up in your quest. We will meet again soon. In the meantime, may good fortune protect you.' Suddenly there was the sound of running steps outside, and Freda burst in through the large doorway of the boathouse.

'Quickly!' she said breathlessly, 'the Bandero Captain has risen. He will be abroad directly. You must leave at once.'

'Go!' yelled Calvos, slapping the rump of Gwen's morsk. There was no time for any further goodbyes, as Herstan and Dreyfus flung the doors of the boathouse wide open. First Gwen, then Meeshka and Polka side by side, then Clumber, and finally Terry, rode out of the shed and into the grey drizzle of a restless dawn.

A visit from the Baron

Castle Turuk was an enigma. A stern forbidding fortress, perched on a tiny island. The battlements belonged only to the swifts, who skimmed around the upper turrets, screaming as they passed. How and when it was built, and by whom, had either never been recorded, or had been carefully removed from all the written records. It was not even known from where the stone was quarried, let alone how it had been transported across the treacherous spill of the falls, and onto the steep and barren rocky island. The castle library contained many ancient tomes, but not one of them held any reference as to how such a feat could have been accomplished. The castle was there, and had been there, for many centuries. But *how* it got there remained a complete mystery.

As a fortification, it was unusual in many respects. Its

unique position and restricted access made all the usual defensive structures of a castle redundant. There was a gatehouse of sorts, but no portcullis. Instead, a reinforced doorway the width of three men abreast was the only entrance to the castle. Storming it was impossible because the suspension bridge, linking the castle to the mainland, could only safely support four or five men at once. Arrow slits were cut in the wall facing the bridge, but nowhere else, because assault from any other direction was unthinkable. The sheer stone walls rose up several hundred feet from the rock, forming at their summit, a more or less rectangular walkway around the perimeter of the castle ramparts. These walls did much to shelter the interior structure of the castle from both the worst of the weather, and the constant noise of the falls. Their main function though, was to ensure that entry to the castle could only be made by the single gatehouse doorway, and thus, absolute control of who entered or left the castle could be maintained. Even if this single gateway into the castle were to be breached, potential invaders then faced two hundred steps up a rather narrow stairway, in order to reach the outer ward. They could be picked off one by one as they came out at the top, assuming they had survived the unpleasant surprises that lay in wait for them on their journey up the stairs.

All in all, Baron Hart had good reason to feel comfortable that his castle was impregnable. No prisoner could cherish any hope of rescue or escape, and the Baron took some pleasure in allowing them to dwell on this fact. As a rule, he preferred not to get personally involved with interrogations. It wasn't that he didn't have the stomach for such matters, because he most certainly did. It was more because he harboured the notion that, should he actively participate, his authority would be somehow diminished amongst his men. In the case of Hev, however, it was his belief that there were greater things at stake. Consequently, he had decided to make a rare exception.

It was three days since the Baron had made his expectations regarding the capture of the children clear to Captain Tache. Since then, the twice daily despatches he received from the east had fired his frustrations to a point where he felt compelled to act. As a result, he had taken two important decisions. Firstly, he had sent for his most trusted covert officer in the field, and his arrival was expected imminently. Secondly, he had left his beloved Map Room and descended into the deepest depths of the castle for a visit to the dungeons.

Hev had been brought to the castle from Carthag two days ago, and he had discovered the very limited hospitality that the castle dungeons had to offer. Meals were of a somewhat basic quality, but regular at least. The cell was small and damp, and the best that could be said about it was that it was quiet – being in the heart of the castle, the constant roar of the falls was completely muffled. A hammock bed, and a thin layer of straw on the stone floor, were the only comforts it had to offer.

Hev had received no visitors since his imprisonment, and nor did he expect to. He awoke from a restless sleep, and listened with interest to the sounds of an unexpected arrival at the guardroom. The gaoler got a particularly unpleasant surprise when, on opening the outer door to the complex, he found that it was none other than the Baron himself who was making an unprecedented visit to the deepest part of the castle.

Baron Hart impatiently gestured away the gaoler's fawning apologies for being unprepared for his visit, and asked to be shown to the new prisoner's cell.

'Open,' he commanded. The gaoler did as he was told, fumbling the keys in his haste to oblige. 'Should I call a guard to accompany you, sir?

'No, you should not, but you will lock the door again after I enter.'

'Very well, sir. Call if you need my assistance.'

The Baron sneered silently at the ludicrous suggestion that he, the Baron, might need to call on such a minion for assistance. Entering the darkened cell, he paused and took a moment for his eyes to adjust to the lower light level.

Hev was crouched in one corner, his head bowed. As the Baron entered, he looked up slowly. He had never personally seen the Baron before, and was unsure who his visitor was. He heard the gaoler lock the door behind his visitor, and concluded that some form of conversation was about to take place. He did not feel obliged to begin it, so it was the Baron who was first to break the silence.

'You are Hev,' he said, more as a statement than a question.

'Yes.'

The Baron cast a glance around the small uncomfortable cell, taking in the few details.

'You are treated reasonably well?'

'I would prefer not to be here.'

The Baron smiled, with his mouth at least, if not his eyes.

'That could be arranged, if you were a little more cooperative.'

'I have given all the information I possess.'

'Sometimes,' said the Baron with a detached air, 'we know more than we think we know.' Hev shrugged and refrained from comment.

The Baron allowed an uncomfortable silence to develop before speaking again.

'You may not be aware that I am Baron Hart.'

'I was not. Perhaps you have come personally to apologise for my unjust arrest?'

'Have a care! I approve of a strong spirit in a man, but you come close to overplaying your card.'

'Well then, may I respectfully ask the Baron the true purpose of his visit?'

The Baron listened for a trace of sarcasm in Hev's answer, but detected none.

'My men have been unable to locate your wife,' he said bluntly. Hev looked the Baron straight in the eye, in a way that few men dared to do.

'That is a surprise to me,' he replied coldly, but inside his heart sang. 'I can only hope no misfortune has befallen her.'

'How do you explain her disappearance, and that of the children?'

Hev decided to gamble. He knew that the Baron was playing a cat and mouse game with him, trying to tease information out. Being locked up in the dungeons for two days had given him plenty of opportunity to think. He had known from the moment of his arrest that Gwen would go north to Piree, and enlist the help of Herstan and Freda. He hoped that the Bandero had gone east or south first of all, and that would have given Gwen the time she needed to reach Piree unheeded. The information from the Baron that she had not been found confirmed his theory.

'Have your men searched the south canal?'

'I ask the questions,' replied the Baron with a glint of steel in his eyes.

'My explanation for my wife's disappearance is simply that we shortly have appointments to keep with merchants in the south. If my early release seemed unlikely, she would take the boat south to honour these appointments. After all, we need to make our living. I have committed no crime, and she will trust that the justice of Castle Turuk will see me free before much longer.'

'And the children?'

'We parted with the children before my arrest. Neither I nor my wife know their whereabouts or intentions.'

'You tell a credible tale, but it seems unlikely you could spend time with them and learn nothing about their plans.'

'They had no plan. They were disorientated and confused.'

'Why did they seek out your wife?'

'An accident of fate, I suspect. My wife is kind to strangers and fond of children.'

'Indeed? A strange twist of fate then? That they should find *her*, amongst all the people of Carthag?'

'I'm sure there are many others who would have done no less for these children, had they met them first.'

'Possibly, yet..., there is something that makes me judge your tale unconvincing.' Hev looked at Baron Hart blankly. The Baron waited a moment, using the silence to good effect. Then, appearing to give his whole attention to his own finger nails, he said casually 'the third child.' Hev did not reply at once, and he shifted uncomfortably as the Baron watched him closely. 'I do not follow your reasoning,' said Hev at last. His tone was perhaps just a little too casual, and the Baron inwardly noted it. 'Well,' he continued, 'it is credible that the first two children may have come across your wife by chance, but for a third child to do the same – that taxes my belief in coincidence.'

'I think the explanation is straightforward,' replied Hev with more confidence.

'Indeed?'

'The third child did not seek out my wife, but the other two children already with her. I understand that my wife was not even present when the three children first met up.' Baron Hart looked up suddenly from examining his finger nails. 'That is my understanding also. And had she not been warned by someone, my officers would have been able to round up all three of the children in your tower.' Hev saw his chance to wrong-foot the Baron. 'I do not understand your interest in these children, Baron. They are foreigners, that much is clear, but hardly a credible threat to the authority of the Bandero.' The Baron began to get irritated – like Captain Tache before him, he was finding Hev a formidable opponent in their exchange of wits. 'My interest is my own affair,' he answered angrily. 'It is sufficient for you to know that you have displeased me by not handing them over. The price for this will be high.'

Hev simply shrugged once more. 'I have done only what any loyal citizen of the Realm would have done. The children are nothing to me, and I can tell you no more. You must do as you see fit with me.'

The Baron was annoyed, not because he felt that the prisoner was lying, but because he wasn't *sure* that the prisoner was lying. Ironically, it was clear that either Hev truly knew nothing at all, or else he knew a great deal.

There was much the Baron could do to make life even more unpleasant for his prisoner, but he was very aware that if Hev was innocent, then his arrest, imprisonment, and suffering would potentially cause much unrest in Carthag. The Baron did not want unrest – not at the very time when the Augury's prophecy might be about to come true. Unrest would divert the Bandero's resources, and stifle the flow of information. The Baron, like his father before him, had long resented the dominion held over the Realm by the distant authority of Emperor Cahito. The Baron's father had made the mistake of challenging that authority by force of arms, and had paid with his life. Baron Hart knew that the Bandero Guard, efficient fighting force though it was, would never have the might to successfully challenge the massed ranks of the Emperor's forces. Instead, he hoped to make that challenge through more subtle means. An ancient promise of some secret power, wielded through special stones. To Baron Hart, by accident of fate, had come the chance to unmask this promised power, and perhaps free the Realm from Cahito's dominance, once and for all, leaving the Baron free to do much as he pleased.

Some ten years earlier, when Baron Hart had first taken residence in Castle Turuk, he had decided to extend the castle dungeons. During the subsequent building work, a letter had been found, cunningly concealed in one of the existing cells. Who the letter was intended for was not clear, but it was assumed with some confidence that it had been written by the stranger Yalyf, whilst a prisoner in the castle. The letter became known as the Augury – a prophecy of significant events to come. Within the castle, the existence of this Augury was a closely guarded secret, known only to a privileged few. It was kept in a secret compartment of the marquetry table, in the castle's Map Room. The Baron, however, had the only copy ever made in the breast copy of his tunic. He stared hard at his prisoner, and took a momentous decision. It was a gamble, without doubt, but if Hev knew more than he was admitting to, sharing this letter with him might just flush that out.

'Gaoler! A torch.'

'Certainly, sir!' came the reply, and a few moments later the cell door was unlocked, and a flaming torch was passed through to the Baron. The gaoler gave a vulgar chuckle as he did so, misinterpreting the Baron's intentions. 'You may go!' snapped the Baron curtly. Hev regarded the Baron with alarm, also unsure as to why the Baron may have made his request. 'Relax, prisoner,' said the Baron brusquely, 'you are not about to be tortured – not yet at least.' The Baron strode over to Hev, crouched in the corner of the cell, and holding the torch above him to give him the necessary light to read by, he handed him the copy of the letter. 'What do you make of this?' asked the Baron innocently. Hev studied the parchment he was handed.

You were only a child when first we met, but do you recall what I said to you then? Sometime in the future, a boy is coming to this land, and his destiny is to gather seven stones. Your destiny is to help him. The seven must be put in place together. Only then can the castle become what it was built for. The boy will understand when the time is right. So will you.

Having read the letter twice, Hev looked up innocently to the Baron. 'This means nothing to me,' he said convincingly, but his mind was racing.

'Come now,' said the Baron encouragingly, 'you must have heard talk of a stranger in these parts, many years ago? And mysterious stones of power?'

'I heard the tavern talk, yes,' agreed Hev. 'I did not pay it much heed. It was, as you said, many years ago.'

'And now that you read what I have shown you?'

'I do not understand its meaning.'

'Perhaps not entirely, but plainly it is the stranger who wrote this. And he speaks of a boy to come.'

'Such rumours are common place. A serving wench could have written this in jest.' The Baron frowned in exasperation. 'I think not!' he snapped. He was frustrated and disappointed by Hev's apparent lack of interest, but he was reluctant to abandon his gamble. 'Who do you suppose the note was intended for?' he asked.

'Clearly someone who was a young child at the time the stranger was here. But as the Baron will surely know, there must be many indeed.'

'Over one thousand in Carthag alone, we estimate,' agreed the Baron. 'I was hoping you may be able to narrow the odds for me.' Hev shrugged. 'I'm sorry Baron, I cannot.' His voice sounded casual, but his mind was frantically trying to judge the likelihood that the letter had been written for Gwen. Certainly, Gwen had met the stranger as a child, but surely so had many other children?

Baron Hart was watching Hev closely. For all the prisoner's replies were convincing, there was something about his manner..., a hint of suspicion. He decided on one last attempt to lure him into revealing the true extent of his knowledge.

'What do you suppose it means by the castle becoming what it was built for?' he demanded curtly.

'I could not say,' confessed Hev truthfully, 'I would have thought that the Baron and his colleagues would be better placed to answer that.' Again the Baron frowned, but this time, more unpleasantly. Hev felt that further comment was expected from him. 'Where did this parchment come from?' he asked lightly. This was a mistake, for the Baron's mood turned suddenly.

'I told you that I ask the questions!' he yelled, slapping Hev's cheek savagely. Snatching the parchment back, he strode purposely to the cell door, and banged angrily to attract the gaoler's attention. While the latter fumbled nervously with the keys, the Baron took one last look at his prisoner, sprawled on the meagre carpet of straw in the corner.

'Do not believe that you succeed in your deception. I tire of this game for now. You need a few more days down here to loosen your tongue further. Reflect on the fact that you may walk out of my castle at any time, once you have told me all that you know.' The gaoler had opened the door, and the Baron turned sharply on his heels and marched swiftly from the cell, his slight limp becoming apparent as he moved quickly. He climbed the steps up out of the dungeons two at a time, and made his way briskly back through the maze of corridors that led to the Map Room. His expression was enough to warn any servants who encountered him that now was not a good time to bother him with any triviality.

As Baron Hart approached the Map Room once more, his pace slackened somewhat, and there was a noticeable easing of the tension in his face. He was back in the area of the castle he felt most comfortable in. He turned the final corner and noticed immediately that the heavy studded oak door to his sanctuary stood ajar. It was unprecedented for anyone to enter the Map Room without the Baron's permission. He paused cautiously in the doorway, conscious that his approach must have been heard by the intruder. Somebody was sitting comfortably in his ornately carved, leather upholstered, armchair. They had their back to the doorway, but he recognised the walnut coloured bald scalp of his most trusted spy. The chair was mounted on a turntable, and as the Baron entered the room, the chair span around to reveal the piercing blue eyes of its occupant.

'Good Evening, Mozz,' said the Baron, now calm once more. 'I have been expecting you.'

North by Morsk

Clumber avoided the main route out of Piree to begin with. There were several alternative trails that, although not as direct, were much quieter. This way, they were able to make good use of the daylight, travelling at full gallop when the terrain was suitable. Their plan was to get as far from Piree as possible in the first few days. Clumber was very familiar with the northern wolds, so it was no problem to bypass the few small settlements on their route, simply taking detours around them. Their progress was so good that by the third night, they had moved into more or less uninhabited territory. Here, they felt confident enough to light their first campfire, albeit in a sheltered hollow, well away from the main trail. During the day, they had met only the occasional herdsmen, driving their cattle or goats to the winter pastures further south. These men, solitary by nature, greeted them with a curt nod, and did not trouble them with any conversation. Of the Bandero, there was no sign.

As they moved off the Great Plain of Carthag and into the northern foothills, the terrain gradually changed. The crops, hayfields, and lowland pasture, common to the south of Piree, was replaced by a coarser, upland pasture, where the autumn had a firmer grip on the land. Frequent freshwater tarns, dotted here and there, allowed them to keep their water-skins topped up, and also provided the luxury of a good wash. Then on the fourth day, they began to notice further changes in the land around them. Rocky escarpments rose and fell away on either side of the trail. Trees were fewer, and more weathered, and grassy peat-bogs filled the deeper hollows. The land overall was rising more steeply, and by the end of the fourth day, they got their first glimpse of the distant mountains, the white tops of which were tinted silky pink by the setting sun. 'Look,' was all Clumber had said. The others nodded knowingly. Somewhere up amongst those mountains lay their destination.

As the land rose, the air became cooler, and the terrain more difficult to navigate. Terry was particularly glad of the warmer clothes and sturdier footwear they had found in the saddlebags. He had retained his waistcoat, with the secret pocket, but he had changed his light sandals for a pair of waterproof boots that were much to his liking.

The fifth day dawned clear and bright, but proved to be a most tedious ordeal for all of them. The trail had dwindled now to nothing more that several intertwining paths, some of which led nowhere in particular. Clumber had been overconfident in her ability to find the way, and twice she had needed to retrace the route. This meant taking them back to a point they had been at an hour previously, to start afresh. It was extremely frustrating, but nobody said anything. Nevertheless, when they stopped to make camp on the fifth evening, everyone was tired and irritable. Even though there was still half an hour of light left, Gwen called an early halt. They found themselves in a broad, undulating valley, through which an icy-cold river snaked and tumbled. Its rushing waters carried the turquoise hue of melt water from the high mountains, so crystal clear that every detail of the rocky river bed could be discerned. A high, featureless blanket of grey cloud had spilled ominously down from the mountains, obscuring any hint of a sunset. Instead, a dreary gloom seemed to condense around them. Saddle sore and exhausted, they slipped off their morsk and sank wearily to the ground.

'Let's get a good fire going to cheer us all up,' said Gwen, trying to revive everyone's spirits as they unsaddled. 'Who will gather the firewood while the rest of us put up the tents?'

'Clumber should have to,' said Polka sulkily, 'she has wasted our time twice today.' Clumber opened her mouth to defend herself, but Meeshka was quicker. 'Polka! Our father would be very angry to hear you speak so. You and I will collect the firewood, and on our return you will apologise to Clumber for your rudeness.'

Polka kicked stubbornly at a clump of grass, but made no comment, and followed his sister meekly enough up the river bank, towards a copse of gnarled trees.

'What is the matter with you?' asked Meeshka as soon as they were out of earshot. 'Clumber is doing her best, and we could not have got this far without her. Don't you understand that it is dangerous for her and Gwen to help us?'

'Why won't Terry answer my questions about his world?' countered Polka, in an attempt to deflect his sister. 'All the time, I ask him to tell me more about the things he talked of on the first day he came here. He still will not say what T.V. is, or computers, or any of the other things I ask about. Why does he deceive us so?'

Meeshka regarded her younger brother in surprise. 'Well, I do not know. But I am sure he has a good reason. In any case, that does not justify your rudeness to Clumber.' Polka bit his lip and said nothing, but nodded quickly once, in reluctant acknowledgement of his wrong. Meeshka's expression softened. 'These are difficult days for us,' she said more tenderly. 'We must think always of what our father and mother would expect of us. You are young still, but you must try. Remember that it is just as hard for Terry — perhaps more so, because the task to find these seven stones has been given to him. Remember also that Hev has been captured, and for all we know, Gwen may never see him again. Yet still she helps us. Our parents would wish us to honour the sacrifices that have already been made. When we return to our world, our people will be grateful to all those in this world who helped us on our trail, including Clumber.'

Silent tears of frustration and guilt trickled down Polka's little cheeks. He turned away, and for several minutes they gathered firewood without speaking. They had wandered quite a distance from the camp, and in the gathering gloom they needed to be very careful. Frequent steep escarpments, stumbled upon unexpectedly, disguised perilous drops of five or ten metres. They edged forward cautiously, often needing to retreat and skirt around a dangerous overhang. As a result, they soon became disorientated, and there was no moon to guide them back. It was only by following the sound of the rushing water that they managed to find the river once again. By then, their arms were full of tinder, so they headed back downstream towards the camp.

Even before they got there, they felt that something was not right. There was an unfamiliar tension in the night air. It was quite dark by now, and they approached the camp warily from behind a large boulder. Silently discarding their firewood, they peered around the rock and down a slight incline, into the hollow where they had left Gwen, Clumber and Terry. It was difficult to make out exactly what was happening in the darkness, but it was immediately obvious that their friends were no longer alone. As they watched, two large torches were lit and placed on stakes in the centre of the camp, picking up the faces of everyone. Three men were rummaging through their saddlebags, carelessly throwing items aside, and shouting occasional reports. Another two men stood guard over their three friends, who were sitting huddled together in front of the tents, with their hands tied behind their backs. Meeshka counted carefully – there seemed to be only five men in total. Although clearly hostile, they did not look like Bandero. None of them wore the standard green tunics and blue capes of the Bandero, and they seemed scruffy and undisciplined.

'Oh Polka,' whispered Meeshka, 'what has happened? Who are these men?'

Polka simply shook his head, staring intently at the scene, taking in all the detail. Suddenly, one of the men threw an empty saddlebag away in disgust, and walked over to the tents and snarled some questions at Gwen. Meeshka and Polka could not make out what was said, but the man was clearly not satisfied with Gwen's answers, for he kicked out savagely at her legs, clumsily missing his target. After a flurry of colourful curses, he turned and barked some orders at the other men. The four of them stood sullenly for a moment, but then split into two pairs. One pair set off south down the river bank, away from Meeshka and Polka. The other two, however, turned north, coming straight towards the boulder that the two children were crouching behind.

'Polka,' whispered Meeshka, 'what shall we do?'

The men were very nearly upon them, so Polka did not reply but pulled his sister down towards the ground and tighter into the boulder. They stayed as still as they could, clinging to the cold stone as the men walked past, not two metres from them.

Clearly both men were unhappy about something, for they were discussing their orders in aggrieved tones.

'How the heck are we supposed to do that?' grumbled one of them to his companion. 'We don't even know who we're looking for, allowing there is someone else to start with.'

'We'll just walk up the river a bit,' muttered the other. 'My guess is we won't find anyone, if yer catch me meaning.'

'I reckon I do,' replied the first man, laughing mirthlessly. 'Then we'll come back and 'ave some merry fun with the prisoners, if yer catch *my* meaning.'

'I reckon *I do*,' snorted the first. The darkness then swallowed them up, and if they spoke again, it did not carry back to the children. Polka waited a moment, and then tugged his sister's sleeve in excitement.

'Listen, Meeshka,' he whispered, 'I have a plan.'

Captured

The five men had taken Gwen, Terry and Clumber completely by surprise. They had ridden in at speed, surrounded them, and tied them up in a matter of seconds. There was a practised air to the way they went about it, with hardly a word being spoken. Their leader was a wild eyed man with few teeth and long, greasy, grey hair. The others referred to him by the name Luke. He brandished a flintlock pistol in one hand, and at his waist, a large knife was sheathed. Terry noticed that the other four men were also armed with knives.

'They are slave traders,' whispered Clumber while the men searched their saddlebags and other possessions. 'They are dangerous,' she added, rather unnecessarily.

'Say nothing,' warned Gwen quietly. 'Hopefully they will leave us alone when they discover we have nothing worth stealing. Terry, is the stone safely in the secret pocket?' Terry said nothing, but nodded ever so slightly. The three of them watched miserably as the men ransacked everything they had. When Luke was satisfied that there was nothing of particular value to be found in the saddlebags, he suddenly rounded on Gwen with an angry snarl.

'Where are the others?' he demanded, the gold in one of his few teeth glinting wickedly in the torchlight.

'What others?' answered Gwen, in a quite convincing fashion given the circumstances.

'Well, when I see five morsk and five saddles,' replied Luke with heavy sarcasm, 'I start to think, maybe there's *five* people. I ain't the best at counting, but I can only make out three of yer so far!'

'We are taking the spare morsk north for two others. They are returning south with us for the winter.' Terry was impressed by Gwen's calmness and resourcefulness under pressure. Luke, however, was not convinced. Kicking out at Gwen in his tantrum, he missed and inadvertently caught a cooking pot, sending it scuttling into one of the tents. He turned savagely to shout orders at his companions.

'Oscar! Ham! Take a walk down the river and look for signs of another two. Rufus and Kern, you two do the same up the river. Don't get taken by surprise! And make sure yer get the better of them!'

Kern, a thick set man with dark, curly hair and sunken eyes, frowned resentfully at this command. 'Maybe the four of us should stick together,' he suggested, 'just in case.'

'In case o' what?' snapped Luke in reply. 'Are yer saying yer can't take a couple o' city brats by surprise in the dark? Not much point in 'aving yer along, if that's how it is! Do as I said!' Rufus shot Kern a warning glance, as if to say *'don't argue with him when he's in this mood.'* Kern shook his head bitterly, but the two of them set off sullenly up the river. Luke turned to glare at Oscar and Ham, who hurriedly nodded and headed south into the dusk, leaving Luke alone with the prisoners.

Luke regarded his prisoners suspiciously. First of all, he checked the three of them were securely bound. He went from one to another, tugging hard at the knots, causing them to wince as the rope cut into their wrists. Then he sat on the ground in front of them, placing the pistol on his lap. Producing a grimy bottle from one of his pockets, he removed the cork with his teeth and took several noisy gulps. This seemed to put him in a slightly better humour.

'How's about a song, me scrawny chickens?' he sneered with contemptuous enjoyment. 'Yer don't look all that 'appy to me! Nowt like a song to cheer yer up.'

Gwen, Clumber and Terry sat huddled together and exchanged anxious glances, but did not reply. Luke surveyed them one by one, and his steely eyes settled on Clumber. A puzzled expression spread over his stubbled face.

'What ye staring at, yer impudent young pup?' he growled, for Clumber had held his gaze defiantly. When she did not reply, Luke spat towards her in a vulgar fashion. 'I reckon I've seen ye afore, young skinny rat-pup.'

'I reckon not,' replied Clumber in a surly tone.

'You watch yer lip! I can soon put that to rights, stinkin' guts of a boatyard rat, I'll say I can!' Clumber shrugged moodily but said no more. Luke's eyes narrowed as he looked at the three of them more closely. 'By the Baron's black blood, what are yer all doing up in these parts anyways? Answer up now, sharply!'

'I've told you,' replied Gwen cautiously, 'we are taking

morsk north. My husband and father await us in the mountains. They have been panning for gold through the summer.'

'You lie,' scoffed Luke, but there was an element of uncertainty in his narrowed eyes.

'I have no reason to lie.'

'There ain't no gold left in them mountains, or I'd 'ave 'ad it meself, long ago. They was panned out years since.'

'I did not say they had found any.'

'Don't try an' be clever with me, missy!' Luke spat again, and wiping his nose on his sleeve, he repeated his assertion more confidently. 'It's a stinkin' lie, an' I know it.' Gwen said nothing but shook her head slowly. Luke patted his sheathed knife with an unpleasant smirk. 'I'll see yer dance to the tune of a hot knife shortly,' he muttered, chuckling to himself in anticipation, 'an' then we'll see how well yer lie, yer stinkin' liar!' He picked up his pistol idly and began to take mock aim at each of them in turn, making as if to pull the trigger.

'Please,' said Gwen desperately, 'we have nothing of value and mean no harm to anyone. What do you want of us?'

'Shut it!' yelled Luke, immediately furious. 'Speak again an' it'll cost the young 'uns a finger each.' He laid his pistol aside, unsheathed his knife, and made mock sawing movements against one of his own grubby fingers. To his delight, both Terry and Clumber looked away in horror.

'Not too keen on the glint o' me blade?' he mocked. 'Let's just test it for sharpness, shall we?' He stood up and made a move towards Clumber. She cried out in alarm and tried to get away, but she was securely tethered to Gwen and Terry.

'Leave her alone,' pleaded Gwen, but just as she did so, Polka suddenly appeared out of nowhere, stumbling into the torchlight. He was crying quietly, rubbing his eyes, and not really looking at anyone.

'Papa's been hurt burying the gold,' he wailed. 'He tripped his self over. I think his leg might be all broke up.' Luke span around like a flipped coin, more at the mention of gold than at the incursion of the small boy. 'Wha's 'at?' he yelled. 'Gold, yer say?' Polka seemed to notice him for the first time. 'Yes, mister,' he replied earnestly. 'My Papa would probably give you some if you came and helped him.'

Luke spat seriously at the ground and considered his predicament. He cast a glance over the prisoners, and then at Polka, who had started to wander back into the night.

'You, young 'un, wait up!' He sheathed his knife, and retrieved his pistol, waiving it menacingly at the three bound captives. 'Don't none of yers move, or it'll be the worse for this young 'un, an' his Pop. Mark my words, yer better be here when I get back!' He paused a moment to sneer at Gwen. 'Panning for gold in the mountains, eh? There'll be a lesson to teach ye when I get back!' Checking his pistol was cocked ready for firing, he trotted off after Polka saying 'I'll help yer Pop young 'un, you just show me where the gold is.'

Fortunately Gwen, Terry and Clumber had been left speechless by Polka's sudden appearance and piece of pantomime, otherwise they might easily have upset his plan. As soon as Polka and Luke were out of sight, Meeshka appeared out of the darkness behind them, and started frantically untying the knots which bound them.

'We must be quick,' she said breathlessly, 'we need to

get everything together, and then we must leave and take their morsk!'

'What about Polka?' asked Gwen urgently.

'He will be back shortly. We must be ready for him. There isn't time to explain, the other men may return any moment.' Meeshka had a talent with ropes, and although Luke had used some cunning knots, her deft fingers soon had all three of them untied. Hurriedly, they gathered their tents and ransacked provisions, stuffing them back into the saddlebags any which way they could, and bumping into each other in their haste.

'Clumber, you get their morsk!' urged Gwen, as they desperately began to re-saddle their own animals. The men's morsk were tethered to a gnarled old tree by the river bank. Clumber unsaddled them, and took great pleasure in throwing both the men's saddles and their bags into the fast flowing river. The current took them out of sight in seconds. Then she took each animal in turn and tied it to the saddle harnesses of one of their own morsk. By the time all of this was accomplished, the others had got everything else packed up.

'Have we missed anything?' asked Terry, casting his eye around the campsite.

'I don't think so,' replied Gwen nervously.

'We must watch out for the other men coming,' whispered Meeshka. She and Gwen climbed up into their saddles, whilst Terry and Clumber took a torch each in one hand, gripping the halters of their morsk tightly in the other. Meeshka held the halter of Polka's morsk, ready to release it when he returned. There seemed nothing else they could do until then.

Where but a moment ago time had rushed, now it

seemed to drag horrendously as they waited for Polka to appear out of the night. Every second was an agony to endure. They could see very little outside the circle of light cast by the torches, and this heightened their nervousness, knowing that it could be the other men who suddenly appeared out of the blackness surrounding them, instead of Polka. The ten morsk seemed aware that something was afoot, for they began shaking their antlers and stamping their feet nervously.

'I don't like this,' said Terry suddenly, 'those other men could easily take us by surprise again. We wouldn't see them coming.' He seemed to reach a decision, and quickly handed his torch to Meeshka. 'Hang on to that a sec, Meesh. I'm going up the river a bit to watch out for those two coming back. I'll come running back as soon as I see them. If Clumber does the same down the river, then at least that way, we'll get some warning.'

'Great idea!' said Clumber enthusiastically, handing her torch to Gwen.

'OK,' agreed Gwen, 'but don't go far. If Polka comes, I'll whistle twice. Come straight back.'

Terry set off into the darkness. Almost immediately, he found he could see further, now that he was away from the light of the torches. The night was ominously silent, but for the sound of his own hurried breaths. He could feel his heart hammering in his chest again, and he remembered that this was just how he had felt when he entered the Huntsman's Cottage, back in Crow Wood. That night seemed a long time ago now. He stopped at the same boulder that Meeshka and Polka had hidden behind earlier, and decided that it was as good a vantage point as any. He settled down by the side of it, and anxiously scanned the darkness in front of him. He could hear the river, away to his left – the sound of it seemed to carry far in the cool night air. For several minutes there was nothing else to be seen or heard. He was keeping his ears peeled for a whistle from behind, which would have been a very welcome sound, but it didn't come. Then his ears caught something. He wasn't sure at first, for the tinkling of the river rose and fell, blending all sounds into one. But then he heard it again. This time it was unmistakeable – the sound of two men, conversing in lowered tones. They were not close enough for him to be able to make out what they were saying, but they were getting closer. He had no doubt that it must be the two men returning from their search, so without any hesitation, he slid quietly away from the boulder and started to run back towards the two torches, which he could still see flickering in the distance. In his haste, he tripped and fell heavily to the ground, letting out an involuntary groan as the breath was knocked out of him. He rolled several times on the slight incline, but he was up and running again in no time. Instinctively, he had put his arms out to break his fall, and his hands had smacked into a slab of stone. His palms were stinging from the impact, but fortunately his legs felt OK. When he reached Gwen and Meeshka, they gasped with surprise at his sudden appearance out of the surrounding blackness.

'They're coming!' said Terry breathlessly, clambering up onto his morsk.

'Oh, Gwen, what shall we do?' asked Meeshka helplessly, tears sparkling in her eyes.

'How far off are they, Terry?' asked Gwen urgently.

'Less than a minute!'

Gwen turned around and whistled twice into the night

behind them. At the same moment, out of the darkness to her left came a whirlwind of small boy, hurling himself onto the morsk that Meeshka held in readiness for him.

'Polka! Thank goodness!' said Gwen.

'We must go!' replied Polka seriously.

'We can't,' replied Meeshka, 'we are waiting for Clumber. She has been keeping look out behind us.' Now their situation was even more desperate, knowing they had only a matter of seconds before at least two of the men returned. Their heads constantly swivelled first south, for sign of Clumber, and then north, for the inevitable appearance of the two men.

'Where is she?' wailed Gwen frantically. She whistled again, but there was nothing. 'Those men must be nearly here,' warned Terry softly.

'We can't leave her,' replied Gwen.

As she spoke, Clumber literally leapt out of the night, mounting her morsk from behind in one swift and elegant movement. The morsk bucked in surprise, but then settled momentarily. 'Let's go,' she said calmly as the others watched in astonishment. Gwen took a moment to recover from her surprise, but then she dug her heels into the flanks of her morsk. 'Ride!' she yelled. She and Meeshka hurled the two torches into the river as they rode up the bank, and the flames were extinguished with savage hisses. Then the five people and ten morsk began to gather pace. Riding as a single unit, they broke into a gallop at the top of the rise.

For the two men returning from up river, it must have been an unpleasant surprise. They had seen the torches flung into the river, and were now approaching the camp at a trot, anxious to investigate what was happening. They were met by the sound of ten morsk in full gallop, rushing towards them in the darkness. This was the sort of situation guaranteed to shake steadier nerves than theirs, and they readily panicked. Hurling themselves to one side, they stumbled on the rounded stones that lined the river bank, and fell in with a loud splash. Terry, who was riding in the rear, could not help giving a satisfied smile as he rushed past. Then the men, and the river, and the camp, were all just part of the darkness behind them. They rode like fury into the unknown, the blast of cool air on their faces giving the night a life of its very own.

Stories by Starlight

The exhilaration of the escape, and the need to put a considerable distance between themselves and the slave traders, kept them riding north through the night for many miles. They had slowed to a canter as soon as it felt safe to do so, for although morsk have exceptionally good nightsight and ample stamina, it was too dangerous to gallop them over such uneven ground with no moonlight. The risk of a serious fall outweighed all other considerations.

Everybody was very eager to hear how Polka had eluded Luke, so as soon as they were moving slowly enough to converse, Polka told them his story.

'At first,' he began, 'I only planned to lead him away from the camp and then lose him in the darkness. Meeshka and me had nearly got lost ourselves out there, with no moon or stars to help us. The land goes up and down too much, and you can't see very far at all. So I thought I'd tell him that Papa and the gold were just down in some big dip, and then run off. He was asking me questions about how much gold there was, but I was pretending to cry so I just told him there was lots. I said I was sure that Papa would spare a coin, perhaps even two, if he helped us.' Polka paused, clearly savouring the next part. 'But then I recognised a place where me and Meeshka had just been, because there were three boulders together in a line. I knew that just up from there on the left was a sudden drop.'

'I remember it,' interrupted Meeshka excitedly. 'We nearly fell over the edge in the dark!'

'That's right,' nodded Polka, 'so I told him that Papa and the gold were just over there, but that I better check with my Papa first that it would be OK to give him a bit of the gold if he helped us. The man didn't wait for me to do that though, he just went charging forward, fast as he could, and fell right over the edge. I heard a big thud, and then he gave this long moan. After that, he was saying all kinds of stuff, but I didn't stay to listen. I came running back to the camp, fast as I could.'

'That was absolutely brilliant!' said Terry enthusiastically, patting Polka on the back as they rode.

'Indeed it was,' agreed Gwen happily, 'we were in quite a fix back there. It was wonderful when Meeshka just appeared out of the darkness and started untying our knots.'

'Sure was,' added Clumber. 'Believe me, there ain't nuthin' good about bein' in the company of slave traders like them. I reckon I've come across that Luke before, when I was just a little 'un. I seen 'im lookin' at me, sort o' strange. I reckon he was trying to place me. Runnin' into 'im was a right bad piece of luck.'

'Well thanks to Polka, he won't be going far tonight,' said Terry happily.

'I chucked all their stuff in the river,' chuckled Clumber, 'so I reckon it's gonna be a cold night for all of them. Specially the two that fell in the river!'

They rode on in contented silence for a while, and then Meeshka cleared her throat, and said rather formally, 'Polka has something else to say, I think.' She nodded seriously at her little brother, who shifted uncomfortably in his saddle, and then turned towards Clumber. 'I spoke unkindly before,' said Polka, hanging his head in shame. 'I am sorry, Clumber, for my rudeness to you.' Meeshka nodded once more, this time in satisfaction.

'S'alright,' said Clumber, deeply impressed, for she was not used to receiving apologies. 'You jus' keep gettin' us out of fixes like that,' she continued, 'an' I'll be happy enough for all of us!'

When they finally stopped to camp again, it was very late. They moved well off the trail, and unpacked only what was essential for the night. They did not light a fire, just in case the slave traders were pursuing them on foot. They took it in turns to keep watch, but the night passed uneventfully.

The following morning, they woke to a grey and chilly dawn, with the tops of the higher peaks dissolving into a misty layer of featureless cloud. There was no wind, at least, but the air was mountain air, and it had a cool sharpness to it. Terry and Polka managed to tickle two fat trout from the shallows of the river that still meandered some distance from their camp. After some discussion, they decided to risk a brief fire to cook the fish. They kept a careful watch from the crest of a nearby ridge, and were able to enjoy a satisfying, if rather hurried breakfast. Then they packed up without delay and set off north again.

'Them slave traders would 'ave smuggled us south, most likely,' said Clumber after they had been riding for a short while. 'When I was a nipper, I got meself sold to one of them southern merchants. They 'ad a house made o' marble, right on the beach. You could 'ear the waves, on a night – I liked that, an' the fact that it were always warm. The Master were always away, but the Mistress, she kept me busy alright. She were nicer than them slave traders though.'

'I'll say one thing for the Bandero,' said Gwen ruefully, 'they don't tolerate the likes of those slave-trading rogues around Carthag. It's more lawless this far north. We must be sure to keep a better guard in future.'

'How much further to this ravine,' asked Terry. Gwen looked questioningly at Clumber. 'It ain't far now,' Clumber said confidently. 'The river's gotten shallow just lately, an' as far as I remember, it ought to be less than a day's ride from here. We need to look out for where the river splits itself into two little becks. The sunrise side 'un, well that comes straight down from the ravine.'

'What happens when we get to the ravine?' asked Meeshka.

'We need to find the Watcher,' answered Terry. 'We must ask them about the clue that Polka solved. And a lot more besides. Mozz told me that the stranger had said that one day, I would understand why all this was happening. I'm hoping that the Watcher will be able to explain a lot of it to me.'

By midday, it was clear that the five morsk of the slave traders were slowing their progress over the difficult terrain.

Whilst their own morsk could be coaxed over difficult sections, the rider-less ones tended to show more reluctance, even stubbornly digging in their hooves in places. Meeshka was very nearly unseated when the animal she was leading suddenly yanked back on its halter, and at that point they reached a decision to abandon the spare morsk. They did not need them for any purpose of their own, so they crossed the river, now that it was shallow enough to do so, and released them on the western bank. Their hope was that even if the morsk wandered back south towards their original masters, the river would prove too treacherous an obstacle further south for them to cross over and be reunited. Once released, the morsk settled immediately into grazing the area where they had been left. When the party moved off, the animals raised their heads just once in curiosity, and then returned their attention to the grazing. They made no attempt to either follow or head back southwards.

'Let's hope they just stay there,' said Terry optimistically, as they crossed back over the river and pressed on towards the ravine.

They found now that the land was changing once more. On both sides of them, the slopes rose to more imposing heights. Immense cliff faces, stained black by the growth of lichen, towered over them in what felt like stern disapproval of their passage. And silvery waterfalls gushed from the upper reaches, tumbling hundreds of feet to become little more than misty filaments of vapour when they finally splattered to the ground. Occasionally, between two summits, they would catch a glimpse of even higher peaks beyond – the true mountains – soaring upwards and glistening white with pristine snow.

At twilight on the sixth day, the river split into two streams, just as Clumber had predicted. They made their camp between the two of them, carefully concealed behind some large rocks. They were still nervous about pursuit, and agreed that they would again mount a watch from a good vantage point. They decided to take the watch in pairs in order to help each other stay awake – other than Gwen – she unselfishly insisted on taking the first shift alone. The four exhausted children gratefully settled down by the fire, and were soon all asleep, for the rigours of the ride north were beginning to take their toll on each of them.

It was late into the night, and long after her turn should have expired, that impending sleep forced Gwen to wake Terry and Meeshka and ask them to take over. The last flicker of the campfire licked the night air and faded, as Meeshka and Terry climbed up to a ledge above their camp that offered both a good view south and some shelter from the elements. They draped a single blanket over both their shoulders, for the night air was very cold. With the coming of darkness, the high cloud cover that had lingered miserably all day, had finally lifted. Staring upwards, Terry and Meeshka discovered a night sky that was silently buzzing with stars. Terry had never known a sky so full. Although he lived in the country, he knew that the light from nearby cities spoiled his view, even on the clearest of nights. Here though, there was no such problem. Eagerly, he sought out the familiar patterns, his eyes welcoming them like friends from home.

'That big W,' he said, enthusiastically pointing to one of the constellations, 'back in my world we call that Cassiopeia.'

'What does that mean?' asked Meeshka. Terry hesitated,

nonplussed for a moment by the question. 'I don't know,' he admitted lamely.

'Well,' replied Meeshka, 'in our world we call that Makushnu. It means *the mountain that is always there*, because unlike some star-families, we can see it the whole year through, so long as the sky is clear.'

'You must live in the north,' said Terry excitedly. 'It is the same in my world! We can see Cassiopeia all through the year from where I live.'

Meeshka nodded. 'But Makushnu also has a deeper meaning,' she continued seriously. 'It reminds us that even though there will always be problems to overcome in life, you should not live in their shadow. Makushnu casts no shadow.'

'I like that,' replied Terry thoughtfully. He swept the sky once more with eager eyes, and pointed to a small cluster of stars that had risen over the steep mountain peaks. 'My favourite constellation is that one,' he said. 'We call it the Seven Sisters, but I can only count six stars, so I don't know why it is supposed to be *seven* sisters.'

'We call that one the Little Wolf Pack,' replied Meeshka with a knowing smile.

'Do you have a story about it?'

She nodded earnestly. 'When the world began, every wolf that lived was in the same great pack. The leader of this pack was a wise and noble wolf called Alkyn, and all the wolves revered and respected their trusted leader. But secretly, some of the wolves were jealous of Alkyn, and they talked amongst themselves about starting new packs. They could never agree who should be the leader of the new pack, so it came to nothing. Alkyn got to hear that a lot of the wolves were discontent, so he called the whole pack together for a great meeting under the full moon. Alkyn stood in the Moonpool, and asked all the wolves to form a line and walk past him. As they did so, he patted every seventh wolf on the nose with his paw. Then he told them that every wolf he had patted on the nose was the leader of a new pack. They must choose whichever other wolves they would like to be in their pack, and then go out into the world and find their own territory. There was great excitement amongst all the wolves, and the new pack leaders raced around, trying to persuade other wolves to join their pack. It took all night, but eventually every pack was sorted out, and they sped off into the dawn to find a new territory. But when Alkyn looked, there were five wolves remaining. He asked them why they had not joined one of the new packs, and they told him that none of the new leaders had wanted them. Alkyn told them that he would like them in his new pack, if they would be willing to join. The five wolves were overjoyed, and they formed a new pack under Alkyn's leadership. Even though it was a very small pack, out of all the new packs it was the strongest, the most successful, and the longest lived.

'And this you can still see, up in the night sky,' concluded Meeshka, 'because although it is a small group of stars, it burns brighter than the other groups. Even though your eyes can wander over the whole sky, they are always drawn back to this one little group of stars.'

Terry looked up, and saw that what Meeshka had said was true. Although his eyes roved from north to south, east to west, they were drawn in the end to the one little star cluster, burning bravely amongst the other giants.

'What do you think the story means?' he asked.

'Well, my mother told me it tells us many important

things. One thing it says is that you don't have to be big to be strong. The strength of the pack is counted not by the number of wolves in it, but by the spirit of those wolves, and the love they hold for their leader. Also, it tells us that a leader cannot be successful unless his pack *wants* to be led. Then there were the wolves that nobody wanted – they turned out to have qualities that had not been recognised before. The story shows us that the best leaders will know the strengths of their pack – strengths that lesser leaders will miss.'

'Well,' said Terry, 'I like that story. I think the people in your world have done a much better job of naming all the constellations.' Meeshka said nothing for a while, but then she asked Terry a question that had been weighing heavily on her mind.

'Why don't you like to talk about your world, Terry?'

Terry looked down uncomfortably. 'What do you mean?' he asked quietly.

'Always Polka is asking you questions about your world – he is so keen to learn new things. He asks you about electricity, and computers, but you give away so little. It is as if your world somehow shames you.' Terry drew a deep breath. He considered carefully before responding.

'It isn't that I'm ashamed of my world,' he began hesitantly, 'but it's not that easy to explain.'

'I will listen, if you will try,' said Meeshka calmly.

'Well, things in my world are very different. In some ways life is more comfortable, because of inventions like electricity. But in other ways, you could say that we've made a bit of a mess of our world. Polka is interested in the useful things, like computers, but not everything is good. There are other things, like pollution and global warming, that harm our whole planet. Technology is great in some ways, but it can be bad for the environment.'

'I don't understand,' replied Meeshka. 'What is technology?'

'Well, it's lots of things. For example, we can talk to somebody on the other side of the world, just like you and I are talking now, using something smaller than your hand. It is called a mobile phone. And I can talk to lots of my friends at once, wherever they are, using something called a computer. We can travel thousands of miles through the sky in something called an aeroplane, in just a few hours. And we have these machines called cars that could take us from Carthag to this ravine in just one day, if there was a proper road to drive on. These are just some of the things that make my world different. So, now that I've said all that, please tell me what you are thinking, Meeshka.'

It was Meeshka's turn to consider her answer carefully. 'I would say that..., that I cannot see how such things could be possible, not in any world.'

'Well then,' sighed Terry, 'now you understand why I don't wish to talk about my world. I could tell Polka all these things and much more, but he would only think me a liar, just like you do. I think that this world and your world are not so very different. You and Polka have always seemed more comfortable here. But for me, this world is more like my world was many years earlier, before things like electricity were invented. It feels like I don't belong here.'

'Well, I do not know what electricity is,' replied Meeshka firmly, 'but I know that Polka and I do not belong here either. We miss our family, and we want to go home too.'

'Sometimes, I wonder if we'll ever get back home

again,' said Terry gloomily, for a cheerless mood had settled on him.

'Of course we will get home again. I will never stop believing that.'

'Well if you believe that, why can't you believe what I'm telling you about my world?'

Meeshka turned and faced Terry, her dark eyes shining in the night. 'Is it true?' she asked solemnly. Terry turned away slightly, feeling suddenly very homesick.

'Yes,' he said, almost in a whisper.

At that moment, from far above them in the sparkling night sky, came the mournful cry of another flock of snow geese. They were hurrying south, driven by a winter that was already gathering its strength in the high mountain passes, not so very far north from where the children lay gazing upwards.

'Well then,' said Meeshka at last, 'I will believe all that you have told me too, although it frightens me to think of such a world. And I will ask Polka not to question you so much.'

'Thanks, Meesh,' said Terry gratefully, hoping that in the darkness, she would not notice the single tear that had trickled down his face. He knew he would feel better in a moment, but there is something about the cry of the snow geese – it speaks straight to the heart of anyone who is far from home. And its message is one of loneliness and failing hope.

The Watcher

They rose at dawn, shivering in the cool morning shadow of the mountains. It felt as if winter had suddenly descended while they slept. The air had a frosty tang to it, which chilled their lungs when they took a deep breath. Above them, the sky was a perfect crystal blue, but the sun was still well below the corniced ridges of the surrounding peaks.

'It's cold,' observed Terry wryly, wrapping his arms tightly around his shoulders and stamping his boots to try and warm the cold toes within them.

'It'll likely be a deal colder, once we get up in the ravine,' replied Clumber, as she struggled to undo the guy ropes of her tent.

'This is not cold compared to winter in Saxonia,' said Polka scornfully.

'It's true,' nodded Meeshka in agreement. 'Most years, the lake by our village will freeze over. Then the whole village will come out and fell a tree. We strip the bark to make wooden skates for everyone, and then we play lots of different games on the lake. It is good when the lake freezes.' She spoke wistfully, and Terry smiled encouragingly, because he guessed she was still feeling homesick.

'There is something nice about every season, even winter,' he agreed. 'But right now, I would prefer it to be a bit warmer.'

They made a quick breakfast of herb bread and what Gwen called gallash – a mixture of ground meat, fat and wheat grain. It was not particularly appetising, but it was supposed to be extremely nourishing. They broke camp and headed north-east along the path of the mountain stream – the one that Clumber had predicted would lead directly to the Ravine of Silence. This soon began to rise quite steeply, with frequent short waterfalls that tumbled into small deep pools. These in turn gushed out between boulders and down into lower pools, forming a sparkling cascade of water. Under different circumstances, the scenery would have been enchanting, but they were a strangely sombre group of travellers that morning – each of them silently lost in their own thoughts. They spoke only when necessary. Even Clumber, who would generally be exuberant over the slightest thing, was content to trot along in front. She frequently stood up in her saddle, staring anxiously ahead for some familiar sign of their destination. The others followed mutely in single file, allowing their morsk to pick its own route up through the countless rocks and boulders that littered their path. Terry, who had a keen eye for all wildlife, was struck by its absence from these high passes.

Some dark birds, possibly ravens, wheeled and dived on the winds that swirled around the higher peaks, but otherwise they seemed to be totally alone.

Around mid-morning, the sun finally crested the south-eastern peaks and lifted the travellers out of their chilly shadow. It lifted their spirits also, as it bathed them in a warm and welcome light. Tentatively, they began to chat once more about nothing in particular, although in oddly stilted and subdued tones – it was as if they were wary of causing offence to some unknown listener. Clumber refrained from joining the conversation, staying focused on her task. She urged them onwards, through a land that rose inexorably ahead of them.

'The mountains seem to be all jammed in tightly,' said Polka perceptively, and the others nodded knowingly.

'I know what you mean,' agreed Meeshka. 'It's like one too many mountains have been forced into too small a space.'

There was no horizon now in any direction, and this heightened their sense of enclosure. Also, there was a growing tension in the air, which they all intuitively felt as they climbed higher into the cold and stark landscape.

Shortly after mid-day, as a veil of high thin cloud began to move in from the west, Clumber brought them to a sudden halt. She stood high in her saddle, staring intently ahead for some time. Then she made an announcement.

'We are here,' she commented abruptly.

Everyone looked up in astonishment, for the terrain did not look so very different from that which they had travelled through for some time.

'Are you sure?' asked Gwen in surprise.

'Yes. Look up ahead.'

From a distance, the two peaks in front of them seemed to join into a single massif, but between them a deep narrow gorge had been carved. The lower slopes were merely steep, allowing occasional purchase to plants and small crooked trees which clung precariously to the cracks and fissures in the rock. Higher up though, the sides were sheer and barren, rising precipitously to the upper snowfields of the high jagged summits.

'I don't like the look of this place,' said Meeshka, frowning uncertainly as she studied the entrance to the ravine. 'It looks the sort of place you could be ambushed in.'

'Well, that may be true,' acknowledged Terry, 'but we have not come all this way just to turn around and go back to Piree. We must go in and find the Watcher, whoever they may be.'

As they entered the ravine, everyone was immediately struck by the menacing silence of the place. A silence which seemed to carry an implicit threat.

'Yang Shoo!' yelled Polka defiantly, but his cry was simply returned in a flurry of bitter echoes, each one more desolate than the last. Then the hush came down again and smothered the place.

Progressing further into the ravine, they found it narrowed to just a few metres wide, and even the lower slopes became sheer. The stream had disappeared underground, leaving only a dried up bed. This was strewn with rounded pebbles and timber detritus, bleached white through long exposure to the elements.

Although there were no apparent signs of life, they all had the feeling that they were being watched. 'It feels like a thousand eyes behind me,' said Polka uneasily, and very soon they were all feeling on edge. They stared anxiously up at the oppressive cliffs on either side. Even the morsk were ill at ease, stopping occasionally for no reason and pawing the stony ground.

'How are we supposed to find this Watcher?' asked Meeshka in a whisper, looking warily around as she spoke.

'I think that they will probably find us,' replied Terry soberly.

'Well, everybody keep a good lookout,' warned Gwen.

They continued cautiously into the ravine, and after about a mile they came across a large rounded boulder that partially blocked their path. On the side facing them as they approached, three words had been painstakingly carved into the rock, and they dismounted to take a closer look. The writing was well weathered, but still clearly legible:

STAND
LOOK
HEAD

'Stand, look, head?' questioned Gwen. 'That doesn't make any sense.'

'Perhaps it means we should stand on the boulder and look ahead,' suggested Meeshka.

'No, I don't think so,' replied Terry. 'I've seen things like this before. You have to say the position of the words.'

'How do you mean?' asked Gwen, puzzled.

'Well, the word *look* is over the word *head*, and under the word *stand*. So it says *look overhead and understand*.'

Clumber was already surveying the cliff faces on each side. Something had caught her eye as she scanned rapidly over the sheer escarpments above them. Something white, below the main snow-line. An isolated patch of snow perhaps, clinging to a sheltered hollow? *Or was it?*

'Somebody is watching us!' she yelled out suddenly, pointing excitedly to a ledge, high up on the north-west face. Everyone turned quickly and looked upwards. Sure enough, a figure dressed all in white stood, arms folded, looking down on them. They were seemingly unconcerned by the dizzying drop. For a while, each party simply stared at each other in silence, but then the figure turned and disappeared into a dark recess behind the ledge. A few moments later they re-appeared and started to haul something over the edge, which fell with gathering pace.

'Look out!' yelled Gwen in alarm, and they tried to hurriedly move back down the ravine. In such a narrow space, with five morsk to lead, this was virtually impossible, but Terry soon called a halt to their retreat.

'It's OK!' he said, 'it's just a rope ladder.'

They looked upwards again, and saw that the bundle was unwinding as it fell. The wooden laths clattered like gunfire against the rock face. It came to a sudden jolting halt as it unwound completely, with the lowest lath reaching perfectly to the ground. The considerable noise of the ladder's fall had stirred a flock of the black birds Terry had seen earlier. They rose from perches around the ledge and swarmed in a raucous and energetic cloud of alarm.

The white figure on the ledge had disappeared back into the cliff face, and the five of them were left to make up their own minds as to how to react to the obvious invitation. 'That must have been the Watcher we seek,' said Meeshka, voicing everyone's thoughts. 'What should we do?'

'I think we are meant to climb up,' answered Terry.

Gwen, who was used to the towers of Carthag and the flimsy corsas between them, looked doubtfully at the climb.

'It is a long climb,' she said uncertainly. 'I hope the ladder is well made. Perhaps we should go one at a time.'

'Well then, I had better go first,' said Terry bravely. He was used to climbing trees and had a fairly good head for heights. Before anyone could object, he placed his foot on the lower rung and began to climb. 'Be careful,' said Meeshka nervously.

Terry soon found that his weight made the ladder hug the rock face, making it difficult for his hands and particularly his feet to get purchase on the rungs. Several times his toes slipped off the rung, and he was left frantically scrambling for a foothold. After about ten metres, however, he discovered it was easier to use an abseiling technique. He pulled the ladder away from the rock and planted his feet squarely against the face. It felt more secure to be walking up the rock, and in this manner, he was able to make much faster progress. Clumber had the presence of mind to grab hold of the bottom of the ladder, which had begun to swing about wildly when Terry changed to the abseiling technique. With the bottom rung firmly anchored, Terry found that he swayed about less, and the climb felt much safer.

As he neared the top, the last few feet became very difficult to climb again because the anchoring of the ladder on the ledge made it harder to separate it from the face. Terry became suddenly aware of the immense drop below him, and felt the panic start to well-up inside. He gripped the upper rungs tightly, and scrambled blindly with his feet for a solid platform. To his great relief he found that a broad ledge had been carved into the face, precisely to help a climber in his predicament. With both feet secure on this, it was an easy matter to reach over the main ledge and haul himself onto its safe haven.

He lay there for a moment on the cold slab, breathing deeply and recovering from the climb. A steady cool breeze whistled over his body, chilling the sweat on his forehead. When he looked up, one of the black birds stood not a metre away on the ledge. It was similar to a Jackdaw, but instead of a silver hood, it was iridescent green, like that of a starling. The bird cocked its head and regarded Terry with one unblinking eye. Then by the simple act of opening its wings, it was lifted effortlessly off the ledge on the breeze. It gave a warning 'chackerchack' as it banked and swooped down out of sight.

Terry rose unsteadily to his feet and saw that the broad ledge he stood on extended back into the cliff face. A deep cave, completely hidden from below by the width of the ledge, had been carved into the rock. It was only a couple of metres wide at the entrance, but seemed to get wider the further back it went. Terry stood silently, watching and waiting to see if anyone came out of the cave. No-one did. The chill breeze continued to blow, as Terry debated what to do. Having made the climb up to the cave entrance, there seemed no alternative but to step into the unknown darkness.

He made his move, but stopped after a few metres to give his eyes time to adjust to the lack of light. He saw that a fireplace, together with cooking ledges, had been fashioned in one side of the cave. A chimney had been carved out of the solid rock, presumably rising to an opening higher up on the cliff face. Beneath this, a spit was positioned over the glowing embers of a large fire, and from it hung a rabbit. Terry observed all of this carefully, and then cautiously moved a little further inside the cave. Then he froze.

A middle-aged woman with long, jet-black hair, and dressed in a long white robe, stood before him. Her face was weathered from a lifetime outdoors, but her blue eyes sparkled intensely. Each regarded the other for a moment, and then the woman spoke.

'Welcome Terry. Long have I watched and waited for you to come, just as Yalyf said you would.' As she spoke, the weathered wrinkles of her face relaxed into a smile of welcome.

'How did you know my name?' asked Terry.

'Yalyf told me about you. I know what it is you seek, and I have information and other things to help you.'

'Are you the Watcher?'

Again the woman smiled, and motioned Terry to sit with her at a table, roughly hewn from solid pine. 'There are some that call me that, yes. And it does much to describe my life these last twenty years or so. Day and night, I have watched the ravine, with the help of none but my birds. My true name, though, is Hellaine.' She poured a clear liquid from a jug into two mugs, and offered Terry a drink. He expected it to be just water, and was surprised to find it had a strong flavour, similar to a summer fruit tea.

'We were told to find you,' ventured Terry hesitatingly, after taking a few sips of his drink, 'but there is a lot I don't understand.' Hellaine nodded sympathetically.

'I don't know why I am here,' he continued, 'although I *do* know that I am expected to find another six stones. I have no idea where to look for them, and even if I find them, I don't know what to do with them, or how to get home.'

Still the woman said nothing, but she smiled encouragingly.

'Then there are my friends to worry about. Two of them are like me, they …, they don't belong here either. I need to find a way to help them return to their home.'

Terry paused at this point, waiting for Hellaine to respond. She carefully refilled his mug before she began.

'I do not have every answer for you, for I understand only what Yalyf was able to tell me. Still, there is much I can help you with. First though, it would be wise to get your companions up into my refuge. These are wild and dangerous lands through which you travel.'

Together, they went back to the ledge, and Terry looked carefully over the edge. The drop seemed suddenly much more frightening, and he was glad he had not looked down during his climb. His friends were staring anxiously up, and waved as soon as they saw his head appear over the ledge.

'It's OK!' he yelled down. 'Can you all come up?'

His question caused much discussion at the base of the cliff, but after a while he saw Clumber begin the climb, using the same technique he had used himself. Clumber was wiry and athletic, and had little difficulty making the ascent. In hardly any time at all, her face appeared over the ledge with a cheeky grin on it, and she hauled herself up and over, collapsing in a heap by Terry.

'Gwen's worried 'bout Polka,' she said breathlessly, 'but he reckons he can make it fine.'

'I have a rope we can tie around the small boy,' said Hellaine. 'That way, should he slip, he will be safe.' Clumber, whose sturdy voice was well up to the task, yelled this information down to Gwen. Gwen waved back in acknowledgement, but sent Meeshka next.

Meeshka began the climb confidently, but by half way it was clear she was having difficulties. From both above and below, they watched with increasing concern. Her progress gradually slowed, and about thirty metres below the top, she came to a complete halt. Gwen was shouting advice from below, but it seemed Meeshka was frozen to the rock face, clinging helplessly to the rope ladder and unable to move in either direction.

'I will lower the rope to her,' said Hellaine, and she rushed back into the cave, returning in a moment with a neatly coiled hemp rope.

'I don't think she'll be able to tie it around herself,' said Terry, 'I'm going to climb down to her.' Hellaine belayed the rope to a convenient rock just within the mouth of the cave, and lowered the other end gently down the cliff face.

'Hang on tight, Meesh!' yelled Terry. Pausing only to remind himself not to rush, he stepped gingerly over the edge and began his descent. This time he needed to look down constantly, but somehow the drop was less frightening when you were going down. He could see that Gwen was beside herself at the bottom, pacing anxiously to and fro, and occasionally shouting up comments that were lost on the steady breeze. But he concentrated on Meeshka, who had not moved now for several minutes. The wind was constantly blowing her hair over her face, but she didn't dare loosen her grip on the ladder in order to remove it. Terry manoeuvred until he was just above her, but it was not clear to him how he could best mount a rescue. After some consideration, he called down to her.

'I'm going to have to climb down next to you Meesh! You just stay there and hang on tight.' All Meeshka could manage by way of response was a slight nod. To make matters more difficult, the breeze suddenly strengthened into a wild wind that whistled down the ravine. Every now and then, a shuddering gust would immobilise them both, forcing them to cower in against the rock face and wait until it subsided. An even greater problem though was the cold. It was seeping into their hands and feet, making it harder to keep a good grip on the ladder, and draining the energy from both of them. Terry realised the situation was becoming desperate. He managed to climb down over Meeshka until he was level with her, and although her face was strained with tears, he was heartened to see her turn towards him and force a grim smile. He stretched sideways for the rope, but it was just out of reach. However, Clumber was watching from above and waiting for just this moment. Lying on her belly, with her head and arms over the edge, she began to swing the rope to and fro. At first only the upper section of the rope responded, but she persisted and eventually Terry saw the bottom length begin to twitch, and then swing back and forth. He was soon able to grab it and pull it in towards Meeshka and himself.

'I'm going to tie this around you, Meesh,' he yelled against the wind, 'and then it will feel a lot safer.' Meeshka nodded bravely and loosened her grip just slightly, allowing Terry to get the rope around her body and under her arms. It was no easy task to do this one handed, because he had to keep one arm coiled around the ladder. However, Hellaine was feeding the rope down to him perfectly under Clumber's instructions, and he was able to loop it around Meeshka and tie it securely.

Immediately Meeshka felt less exposed, and was able to relax a little. 'Sorry,' was all she managed to say, but it was enough to show Terry that she would be able to manage the climb alright from now.

With Clumber and Hellaine exerting a slight upward tension in the rope, Meeshka felt confident to begin the ascent again. It felt so much safer with the rope gently tugging her upwards. Terry stayed where he was, anchoring the ladder away from the rock, and Meeshka was soon able to cover the final thirty metres to the top. When she reached the ledge, Clumber and Hellaine hauled her bodily over the lip and into the mouth of the cave. There she lay exhausted, unable to speak for several moments. It wasn't until Terry had climbed back up that Meeshka began to recover.

'Thanks, everyone. I'm sorry I got stuck.'

'That's a tough climb,' replied Clumber generously, ''specially now it's got windy.'

'But you have resourceful friends,' said Hellaine, who beamed at Terry in particular. 'That bodes well for your future task.'

'We better let Gwen know we're all OK,' said Terry. He walked back to the edge and signalled with his thumbs up that all was well, and then Meeshka bravely crawled to the edge and waved weakly down to Gwen, who waved happily back.

Next it was Polka's turn, and Hellaine lowered the rope all the way to the ground for Gwen to tie it tightly around him. Perhaps chastened by Meeshka's experience, he did not seem to object, and stood meekly while Gwen double checked the security of her knots. As soon as Gwen signalled they were ready, Hellaine and Clumber began to pull gently on the rope, and Polka began his climb. Being lighter, it was easier for them to pull him up, and he soon seemed to hardly need the rope ladder at all. He just used his feet to keep himself off the rock face. In record time he was safely up on the ledge and waving cheerfully back down to Gwen.

Before she began her climb, Gwen led the morsk to the leeward side of the large boulder and made them comfortable. She draped a blanket over each and filled their nosebags with meal. Only when satisfied they were well settled did she finally start up the ladder, and as she did so the first swirls of snow came wheeling down the ravine, carried by a north wind that was suddenly bitter. Gwen was determined, however, and she climbed steadily and confidently. When her head appeared over the top of the ledge, her blonde hair was plastered with snow on one side.

Hellaine was first to greet her as she climbed onto the ledge. 'Welcome to my meagre home,' she said. 'You must all come inside, for the winter snow has made its first foray out of the Whitelands.'

Darkness was descending as Terry helped Hellaine pull the rope ladder back up onto the ledge, making their refuge a safe haven from all threats in the night. Then they all retreated into the cave and Hellaine drew a great thick curtain, made from a patchwork of various skins, over the entrance. It proved a very effective barrier, and the wind was left to howl on the outside, as the blizzard gathered its strength. Inside, the large fire was stoked up and roared back in defiance. Hellaine put two more rabbits on the spit, and root vegetables were soon boiling away merrily on a narrow stone slab which extended out over the fire.

'I hope the morsk will be OK,' said Terry anxiously.

Gwen smiled. 'The morsk will be fine,' she said. 'This blizzard will be nothing to them, for they are very hardy.'

'It is true,' agreed Hellaine. 'Further north from here, wild morsk roam free with no shelter from the cruel weather. Somehow they eek out a living from nothing more than the scraps of lichen that grow up there.'

'Well, it is nice to be safe and warm up here in your cave,' said Meeshka.

'You are all most welcome,' replied Hellaine. 'Terry at least, has been expected for a long time now, but it is good to know he has brave and loyal friends to help him. We will eat first, and then it will be time to talk.'

Hellaine's Tale

They sat together around the fire, keeping their feet warm, while their shadows danced and flickered on the walls of the cave. It seemed a long time since they had enjoyed a meal in comfortable circumstances, and the rabbit stew was delicious. They ate hungrily, with little or no conversation, and when they had finished, Hellaine produced hot mugs of herb tea.

Outside, the storm raged – the whine of the wind rose and fell as it sped down the narrow channel of the ravine, plastering snow onto every exposed rock in its path. Despite Gwen and Hellaine's assurances, Terry couldn't help feeling sorry for the morsk, stuck outside in such a blizzard. He was glad to be safely up in the shelter of the cave. The heavy skin curtain that covered the entrance juddered every now and then, but not even the slightest draught managed to penetrate through.

Cradling their steaming mugs in their hands, they settled down cosily on the warm stone slabs of the cave floor. Meeshka lay with her head on Gwen's lap, staring into the depths of the fire, where the embers glowed with sudden surges of bright orange. Without the need for anyone to say so, they all sensed that the moment to talk had arrived.

Hellaine put her mug down and looked seriously at Terry for a moment, before speaking. 'I think perhaps, that to begin with, there will be some questions you will wish to ask.' Terry nodded, and paused to consider where to start. The others gave him encouraging glances, but waited patiently. They knew that they must stay silent, allowing Terry to speak on their behalf.

'First of all,' he began, 'I would like to know who Yalyf is, and how he knew that one day I would come here?'

'I will start at the beginning,' Hellaine said slowly, 'and I will try to tell you everything I know, or have guessed, in the long days and nights since I took up this vigil. But I do not have a full answer to this question. You must understand that Yalyf could not tell me anything that would be of value to the Baron, for fear he would torture it out of me.' Hellaine looked away sadly for a moment. 'He should not have been concerned on that account, for no matter how foul the practises of the castle dungeons, nothing could have persuaded me to break my promise – to tell my tale only to you.' She paused a moment to gather her thoughts, and then began.

'Yalyf came to this land twenty-one years ago. I was working as a shepherdess on the northern plain. A lonely life for a young woman perhaps, but one that suited my nature. One night, as I sat by my campfire, Yalyf appeared out of the darkness. He must have been drawn by the light. He was quiet, and spoke very little at first, seeming content just to have some company. He did not stay long that first time, but in between his wanderings around the land, he returned to visit me several times. It was clear that he was different from other people in these parts, and very soon he became known as the Stranger. Some people shunned him, but others were curious and would seek out his company, even following him when he was alone. Rumours began to circulate about his purpose here, and before long the Bandero became interested. In those days, the Bandero were more under the control of Emperor Cahito, who had many soldiers in Carthag. I have heard that it is different today. The soldiers are gone, fighting wars in the south, and the Baron and his henchmen do much as they please.'

'They have been chasing us ever since we arrived here,' said Terry.

'Well, that was to be expected. The Baron knows part of the tale, for at one time his father held Yalyf a prisoner in Castle Turuk. Perhaps he knows more than I, who can say for sure?'

'How is it that other people seem to know that I and my friends would come here one day?' asked Terry.

'A prophecy like that can not remain a secret. The news was certain to spread, and Yalyf knew that. Indeed, he welcomed it, because he told me himself that you would need the help of all good people if you were to succeed in your quest.'

'What else did Yalyf tell you?'

'He was anxious that I understood that there were parts of the tale he could not tell me. If Baron Hart were to learn of my link to the stranger, then I would not have been left in peace to conduct my lonely watch. So, for my own protection, Yalyf told me only as much as I needed to know, in order to help you when you came. However, I have guessed more, for twenty-one years spent mostly alone is a long time in which to think. I do not believe Yalyf counted on that.'

'Do you know about my world,' asked Terry hopefully.

'Yalyf told me that these worlds are not really different worlds, it is all just one world, but they are different *futures*. You live in one future, and I in another, but it is the same world. You will notice, for example, that the same moon, and the same stars populate the night sky.' Meeshka smiled and caught Terry's eye at this.

'Has Yalyf been to my world?' continued Terry.

'I think he has been to several worlds. Which one he truly belongs in, I could not say, but I do not think it was this one. In each world there is much that is the same, but also much that is different.'

'In my world, there are things that would be considered impossible in this world,' said Terry gloomily.

'Perhaps so. Each future of the world has developed in its own way, for on the spin of a coin can the course of history turn. These matters should not worry you. Your world's future is just as real as the world you find yourself in now. When you have all seven stones, you will be able to return there.'

'Are you sure?' asked Terry eagerly. 'What about Meeshka and Polka? Their world is different again.'

'There is every reason to believe they will return to their world safely also, provided you are able to gather all the stones.'

'What are these stones?'

Hellaine's eyes seemed to light up at Terry's question.

'The stones possess some secret power. Yalyf told me that knowledge of this power would be a very dangerous thing. Again, for my own protection, he could not share it with me, but he did tell me a little about their names and colours. From what you said about finding another six stones, I take it that you already have the first one?' Terry nodded, and feeling inside his waistcoat for the secret pocket, he removed the black bag and took out the amber green tumblestone. He offered it to Hellaine.

'Ah yes, the Hawk's Eye,' she said softly, her eyes shining in the gloom of the cave.

'Do these stones make the person holding them powerful in some way?' asked Terry.

'I am not sure,' she replied, returning the stone to Terry, 'but I do not think they are *magical* stones as such, no more so than a spy-glass is magical. Many believe, however, that the stones can protect you – and others say that they are healing stones. I wish I understood their nature more fully, but I do not. Of one thing I am certain – the importance of these seven stones goes far beyond their ability to protect or heal. What Yalyf feared most was that the stones would be discovered by people who would use them for harm – and this brings me to an important warning he wanted me to give you. Often, he would carry a worried expression, and he would ask me if I had seen shadows.'

'Shadows?' asked Terry, puzzled.

'Yes. He wanted to know if I had seen dark shapes, like shadows, that appeared very suddenly, and then disappeared. Once, he referred to them as the *Sans-Schen*, but he would not be drawn on details. Only from the smallest pieces of information have I been able to put together my guesses. I suspect they do not belong in this world – perhaps they are from some dark and dreadful future of the Earth – I could not say for certain. They crave the stones, for some evil purpose of their own. Yalyf greatly feared that the seven stones would be taken by them, with terrible consequences. Something would happen that reached beyond just this world, harming people in all the other worlds as well. That is why they have been hidden separately, and precautions have been taken to prevent their accidental discovery. It is your quest to find each of them and take them to safety.'

'Why did Yalyf choose me for this task?'

Hellaine shook her head slowly. 'Your connection to Yalyf is something he would not explain to me, although I pressed him frequently enough. *Who is this boy Terry?*, I would say to him, but always he told me that it would be better I did not know who you were, or where you came from. I had thought perhaps he was your father?'

Terry thought briefly of his father, sitting in an armchair with his feet up, and reading the newspaper. He loved his father, but knew him as the least adventurous person that could possibly exist. What little he knew of Yalyf was enough to convince him that there could be no connection with his family.

'No,' he replied with certainty. 'That is not possible.'

'Well then,' said Hellaine, 'that part is to remain a mystery.'

Terry stared hopelessly at the cavern walls for a moment.

'How can we hope to find all these stones?' he asked.

'Clues have been left with each stone to help you find the next one. Did you not receive a clue with this first stone?'

'We did, and Polka has solved it. But we do not yet understand what it means. It was the word CROSSBOW.' Hellaine looked up quickly in astonishment.

'Crossbow, you say?'

'Yes,' explained Polka, stirring from his comfortable position by the fire. 'There was a poem, and you had to take the first letter of each line.'

'Wait there,' said Hellaine firmly. She rose and went to the back of the cave, where she removed something hanging from the wall. She returned with a beautifully carved and polished crossbow. It was obviously the work of a master craftsman.

'This was Yalyf's parting gift to me,' she said with pride. 'He knew that surviving in these barren parts would be no easy matter. In summer, things are not so difficult – I can even grow vegetables up on the plateau. But the winters are hard. My snares stay empty for weeks. This bow has won me many a good meal of snow-grouse and the like when I have been hungry.'

'Why would Yalyf have made this the answer to our first riddle?' asked Terry.

'I don't know,' admitted Hellaine, thoughtfully examining the weapon afresh. 'If that is truly the clue for the next stone..., then...' She held the crossbow up by its sturdy tiller.

'This stock can be removed,' she said, disengaging the crossbow's butt from where it was attached to the rack by a square locking pin. She held the smooth block of wood, about the size of her forearm and hand, aloft for them all to see.

'Could a stone be hidden inside?' asked Gwen.

'It's possible,' agreed Hellaine, 'but the grain of the

wood is unbroken. There looks to be no mechanism for opening this up.'

'Could I see please?' asked Polka. He took the wooden stock and examined it closely. Then placing it end-on, on an upturned saucepan, he began to tap the wood lightly with one of Hellaine's spoons. He moved systematically along its length, listening carefully for any change in tone. He did this several times, and returned always to a point about half way down the block.

'Can you hear that?' he asked excitedly. The others listened intently, and became convinced that the tone of the tap, amplified by the saucepan, was slightly different at the point Polka had brought to their attention.

'I believe there was something else we missed in the poem clue,' Polka announced. 'The part where it said *burn the riddle once you know*. We thought that was telling us to destroy the clue, once we had solved it. But I think it might really have meant this.' He looked up at Hellaine with sombre eyes. 'I'm sure that there is a stone hidden in here, and the only way to get it out is to burn the wood away.'

Meeshka gasped and looked doubtfully at her brother. 'Oh Polka, are you certain about this? It is a lot to ask of Hellaine, especially if this was a gift from Yalyf.'

Gwen too, looked uncertain. 'We will be destroying a valuable possession,' she said quietly, 'we need to be positive before we ask this of Hellaine.'

If Hellaine was dismayed at Polka's suggestion, she did not show it. She gazed reflectively at the stock for a moment, and then without saying anything, she gently took it from Polka and placed it on the glowing embers of the fire. 'We have to know,' she said. 'I can always make another stock, although it may not be as fine as this one.' As the first tongue of flame flickered around the base of the wood, they knew it was too late to change their minds.

It took twenty minutes for the stock to burn through to cinder, and very little was said by anyone during that time. Polka remained confident, keeping his eyes firmly fixed on the burning wood. Terry, Gwen and Meeshka remained subdued, watching with a mixture of hope and fear.

Eventually, Hellaine fished the blackened block out of the ember with a pair of tongs, and dowsed it with cold water. Then she picked it up and examined it carefully. By twisting sections of it in her hands, she was able to crumble the charcoal away. As she worked towards the centre, the whole stock suddenly split down the middle, and a small tin box fell to the floor. Immediately, everyone crowded around. 'Careful,' warned Hellaine, 'it is still hot.' She poured more water over it, until it was cool enough to lift. It took her some time to prise the lid off, but when it eventually came away, a dark blue tumblestone fell out of the tin, together with a piece of paper.

'It is beautiful,' exclaimed Hellaine in delight. 'To think that I have carried it around all these years! Well done to you, Polka!'

'What's on the paper?' asked Terry eagerly.

Hellaine unfolded it and placed it before them for everyone to read.

This stone is Dumortierite. The next clue is:
NEW7
SNOW13
HERE23

'New snow here?' questioned Meeshka as she read

aloud. 'Does it mean we have to go somewhere where there is new snow?'

'No,' said Polka emphatically. 'The numbers will be an important part of the clue. I will solve it if you give me time.'

'We will all think about it,' said Gwen thoughtfully.

'Why do we have to solve all these clues?' asked Terry in frustration. 'Why couldn't Yalyf just tell us where to find the next one?'

'It is a safeguard,' replied Hellaine. 'If the Bandero found a stone somehow, they would very easily find all the subsequent stones as well. Yalyf left clues that he felt the Bandero would find difficult, but that you and your friends would be able to solve. Perhaps he even knew that you would have a good clue-solver with you in the shape of Polka.'

'Well, I suppose that makes sense,' admitted Terry grudgingly.

'Look on the bright side,' said Gwen cheerfully. 'We have two of the stones already, and soon we will find the third. We have come a long way, but we are doing well.' Terry nodded and smiled, his mood lifted by Gwen's optimism. He placed both the stones in the black velvet bag, and returned it to the secret pocket in his waistcoat.

'At least we understand a lot more now,' he said, 'but there is something else I would like to ask – what happened to Yalyf?'

'I do not know,' replied Hellaine sorrowfully. 'His purpose in seeking me out was to find someone he could trust with the information to help you. He needed somebody who lived apart from other people, in a place that was not readily accessible. I'm not sure why this was so, or how he found me. But find me he did, and spent several weeks with me here in the north. Together we wandered alone amongst these mountains, and it was Yalyf who brought me to this cave. I asked him how he knew of it, and he said he had been here once before.'

'How did you climb up,' asked Terry curiously. Hellaine smiled knowingly. 'The ravine is not the only entrance to my grotto,' she explained. 'Yalyf chose this place so that I would have a means of escape, should the Bandero ever come for me. There is a secret tunnel at the back of the cave, which leads out onto a plateau between the mountains. From the north, there is a difficult and concealed trail by which this plateau can be reached. That is how we first made our way here.'

Terry listened to this with interest. 'Why did Yalyf leave?' he asked.

'He said he must return south, to complete one final task. I heard once, from a travelling shepherd, that he was captured by the Baron and held prisoner in Castle Turuk. I do not know what became of him, although I would very much like to.'

'Have you never been lonely, living up here by yourself?' asked Meeshka, and then added coyly, 'if you do not mind me asking.'

Hellaine held Meeshka's innocent gaze and smiled thinly.

'I was living alone before Yalyf found me – it is my way. To some, this must seem a harsh life, but there has been purpose in it. All things happen for a reason. Over many years, I have come to think that I am here because it was needed for me to be here. That has been reason enough, for me.' Hellaine turned to Gwen. 'All the same, I did cherish the hope that when my vigil was finally over, I would learn of Yalyf's fate. Have you no news of him?'

'I met him once,' said Gwen, 'as a child, collecting water from a well. He spoke to me, but I do not remember what was said. I too had heard that he was captured by the Baron, but nothing more. I am sorry, but perhaps it will become clear when the quest is complete.' Hellaine nodded, but there was a far away look in her eyes. For a long time, nobody spoke. Then Terry posed one final question.

'The clue with the first stone said something about *fear the foe*. We had thought that meant the Bandero, but do you think it meant these shadow people?'

Hellaine thought carefully before replying. 'The Baron and his henchmen are formidable foes indeed, and they are the more immediate danger. However, I have to say that I think your suggestion is correct. It was clear that Yalyf knew there was a deeper, darker force at work here. For the Baron to get the stones would be a disaster, but one akin to a pistol in the hands of a babe. Whoever the Sans-Schen may be, I suspect they pose a threat far greater than the Baron, or even the Emperor himself.'

'But who are they?' asked Terry, 'and where do they come from?'

'These are questions I cannot help you with,' Hellaine replied, 'but I can offer you one small comfort – I believe that Yalyf hoped you might never come across them. He feared them, but he did not *expect* them. I would suggest that all you can do is stay alert.' Clumber, who had sat silently through the whole discussion, looked up and scowled menacingly. 'Well, whoever they are,' she said, '*I'll* be watching for 'em.'

Hellaine smiled. 'I see Terry is fortunate to have good

friends on his quest. But it is late, and now is the time for sleep. Let us hope that the storm blows itself out through the night. In the morning, you must continue your search for the remaining stones.'

Terry woke once through the night, coming suddenly awake after a restless dream, in which he had been pursued through waist deep snow by unknown enemies. In the dream, he had been searching frantically for something lost at his feet, but when his toes finally touched some obstruction, and he brushed the powdery snow away, it proved not to be what he sought. Instead, he uncovered a dead morsk, lying frozen solid on the rocky ground, with the light of the moon reflecting in one of its glassy eyes.

As his body recoiled from this gruesome discovery, he came fully awake in the dark cave, and shuddered involuntarily at the memory of his dream. There was silence, and he was comforted at least by the knowledge that the storm had subsided. He rose from under his blanket by the dormant fire and went to the entrance of the cave. Pulling the curtain aside, he revealed a still and beautiful starlit scene. The opposite wall of the ravine had been transformed, for now great clumps of snow clung to the smaller ledges, and higher up and beyond, the fresh snowfields glistened like icing on a cake. The stars above sparkled like diamond studs on black velvet, and as he watched, two meteorites skimmed rapidly across the sky, one after the other in quick succession. Terry was not superstitious, but he couldn't help thinking that they were some sort of omen for the difficult times ahead. Whether good, or bad, he could not decide.

The morning dawned bright and crystal clear once again. Gwen unfurled the rope ladder and went down to the morsk whilst breakfast was prepared. She returned soon after with the good news that all five seemed in good spirits and were restless to be under way.

'The blizzard must have blown itself out quite quickly last night,' she said, 'for the snow is not too deep, at least, not here in the ravine.'

'You will likely find that the snow lessens as you descend back towards Piree,' said Hellaine. 'Winter is barely upon us, and it is early yet for the heavy falls.'

After breakfast, Meeshka had to face the rope ladder once more, and the descent down into the ravine. She had been dreading this moment throughout the night.

'Could we not return by the tunnel, out onto the plateau?' she pleaded.

'Even in summer, it is two day's journey,' replied Hellaine. 'Although the snow will cause you no problems on the trail down to Piree, up on the plateau it will be lying waist deep. I'm sorry, but the journey would be impossible.'

Meeshka nodded miserably, but she did not complain again, and prepared herself to face the ordeal.

This time the rope was tied around her at the top, and Gwen went down just in front of her. Hellaine and Clumber lowered her gently, and in the event, she managed it without difficulty. She leapt off the last rung of the ladder, and those above heard her exuberant shriek of delight, once she was safely down.

Polka was lowered next in a similar fashion, and he too managed the descent with no problems. Clumber declined Hellaine's offer of the rope with derision, and set off in a cavalier fashion. She slipped alarmingly half way down, causing Gwen to cry out in dismay, but fortunately her one-armed grip on the ladder held securely. After this scare, Clumber continued in a more cautious manner and arrived at the bottom in a rather subdued mood.

Last of all came Terry. He stood at the top of the ledge, unsure what to say.

Hellaine smiled warmly. 'Good luck, Master Terry,' she said. 'I have waited a long time to meet you, and you have not disappointed me.'

'Thanks for all the help you have given us,' said Terry earnestly.

'We shall meet again, before all this is over,' said Hellaine, 'I feel sure of that.'

'What will you do now?'

'I have not yet considered that, but I am used to the harsh life up here. I will make no quick decisions.'

Terry nodded. 'Goodbye then, and thanks again.' He turned to begin his descent.

'Wait!' called Hellaine, rushing to the edge. 'There is one more thing.'

Terry paused and looked up expectantly.

'There is something..., something about the castle. I only know what I overheard one night as Yalyf slept. A few words murmured in the dark, but they struck me as significant.'

'What did he say?'

'*They could find the letter.*'

'What letter?'

'I don't know. Not even who it was from, or who it was to. But I think he was worried that the Baron might find it.'

Terry looked up thoughtfully. 'Did he say anything else?'

'Something about the Castle's secret being in danger.'

'Well, I don't understand what that means.'

'Nor do I. I'm sorry it is not much, but I remembered it during the night. I could not say why, but I feel it is important.'

'OK,' nodded Terry, 'I will remember it.'

'Take care, Master Terry.'

'I will try to,' he replied, and disappeared down into the ravine to rejoin his friends, who were waiting anxiously below.

Unexpected News

As Terry was descending the rope ladder back into the ravine, Hev was sitting slumped in the dungeons of Castle Turuk, despairing of all hope. He had had no visitors since the Baron, just over a week previously. The only human contact he had enjoyed during that time was with the gaoler, who he had found to be crude and surly. He had just finished a meagre breakfast of cold porridge when, to his astonishment, Captain Tache arrived abruptly at his cell, barking orders to an equally astonished gaoler.

The cell door was flung open and light from the well lit corridor flooded in, causing Hev to shield his eyes against the unaccustomed brightness. Captain Tache strode purposely into the cell and stared unflinchingly down at Hev.

'I have come to tell you that you are to be released,' he said coldly.

'You have found my wife?' asked Hev.

Captain Tache grimaced momentarily. 'We have not,' he answered tersely. 'It seems your wife is adept at disappearing without trace, and taking a canal boat with her.'

'I trust no harm has befallen her.'

'Difficult to judge, wouldn't you say? You have led us a merry dance, east, south and then north, and all to no avail.'

'And yet I am to be released?'

'Not by my orders, I assure you.'

Hev noted the bitterness in the Captain's tone, and deduced that the order must have come from above.

'In what way then, have I earned the benevolence of the Baron?'

'The Baron's ear has been seduced by others,' snapped Captain Tache. Then realising he had let his anger cause him to reveal too much, he turned briskly and left the cell. 'The gaoler will see you to the gatehouse!' he shouted as he climbed the steps out of the dungeon, slamming the outer complex door savagely behind him. Hev and the gaoler exchanged wide-eyed glances. It was difficult to tell who was the most surprised.

Hev was met at the gatehouse by two junior officers, who told him curtly that a morsk would be provided by the stables. This was only to get him as far as Carthag – the animal must be handed back to Bandero officers at the interrogation centre, immediately upon his arrival in the city. He was then discharged without further comment or explanation. Crossing the perilous suspension bridge over the falls by himself, he stepped gratefully back onto solid land. He looked back just once at the magnificent castle, towering majestically over the permanent mist that was generated by the frothing torrents below. Nobody had followed him. Apparently, he was free to go where he pleased. A morsk was tethered outside the main stable block, and he took this to be the promised animal. He lost no time in climbing up into the saddle, and setting off resolutely on his long ride east, back through the forest towards Carthag.

Hev was unaware that his departure from the castle was actually being watched closely by two people. Baron Hart and Mozz stood high up on the upper walkway, in a tower known as the Donjon. They enjoyed a clear view of the bridge and buildings on the far side.

'You are sure about this?' the Baron asked his companion, as Hev reached the far side of the bridge. 'It has angered my Company Captain greatly to be overruled.'

'We find ourselves in momentous times, Baron. The child that the Augery speaks of has arrived at last. We must handle the situation carefully. The fewer people who know of our plans, the better it will be for us. Had I led your men to the children, that night at the canal junction, we would have lost our chance forever. We would have the boy, but not the stones. We must play our fish carefully – still we do not know who the stranger meant by *someone knows you are coming*. Your men will get their chance, but for the time being, they must follow their orders. More than twenty years I have served the House of Hart – surely I have earned your trust by now?'

The Baron watched Hev disappearing into the forest. 'This is too important a matter to rely on the trust of one man,' he said grimly. 'You will need support, when the right time comes.'

'I agree,' replied Mozz. 'I will follow him alone to

begin with. The boy and his companions will have found the one who waits for them. And he will have learned how to find the stones, I am sure of it. The woman, Gwen, will want to re-unite with her husband before they make their move. The prisoner will lead us to them, and thus to the stones. Then your men may arrest them.'

'How can you be certain of their intentions? It seems to me that you gamble much.'

Mozz smiled confidently. 'Recall that I spent many hours with the stranger, while your father had him imprisoned here. For all he tried to mislead me, still he could not hide the truth from me. The boy and his friends are here to gather the stones.'

'My captain will not understand these tactics.'

'It is best I work alone to begin with. When the picture clears, I will get word to Tache. Keep him some distance behind me, but close enough to give support when required. He understands my role for the House of Hart?'

'He does, but he is the only one of my captains who I have shared that information with. Just be sure that your request for support does not arrive too late!'

'For the most part, Baron, we are dealing with women and children. There is little to fear. Once they have the stones, we can arrest them at our leisure.'

'Yet this same woman and children have proved able to evade an entire company of my men, presently searching for them? That suggests a certain presence of mind, don't you think?' The Baron's bittersweet tone was not lost on Mozz.

'The woman has been lucky, and no-one can be lucky always. In any case, their continued freedom is to our advantage, as I have explained. As for the children, I have taken the boy, Terry, into my confidence. All the pieces are set, we simply need to let the game play out.'

The Baron stared hard at his chief spy. 'Understand this – your plan had better work, or there will be… consequences.' Mozz grinned and his blue eyes sparkled. He enjoyed this verbal sparring with the Baron, but knew when to stop.

'You can be assured I will be giving this matter my careful attention, sir,' he said cheerfully. 'I will give him an hour, and then set off. He will head for Carthag first, I am certain of that. Then we shall see.'

'Very well. You will send progress reports?'

'Of course. Anything significant will be sent with my seal and delivered to your hand.' The Baron nodded curtly, and turned to descend the steps of the Donjon back down onto the terraced lawns, and thence into the heart of the castle keep. Mozz remained on the tower, watching Hev until he disappeared into the golden leaves of the autumnal forest.

The Baron did not return to the Map Room immediately, but sought out Captain Tache in his quarters off the south bailey.

'At ease, Captain,' said the Baron, as he entered Tache's chamber unannounced.

'You are surprised to see me here, no doubt?'

'Yes, sir,' answered Captain Tache cautiously. *Surprised and annoyed* is what he would have liked to have said. He had spent the last week in a frustrating and fruitless search for Gwen and the children. No boat fitting the description had been seen in Piree, and whilst the tavern owner's behaviour had been suspicious, it was not sufficiently so to justify his arrest. Despite personally questioning many others, nobody could recall seeing the fugitives. After leaving Piree he had widened the search, and enlisted more men to re-check all the canals. At one point, his entire company of fifty men had been involved, and still there was nothing. Such a silence was not natural. Reluctantly, Captain Tache had made the humiliating journey back to Castle Turuk, to report his failure to the Baron. Now the Baron was here in Tache's quarters – an event so unusual that Captain Tache could not remember it happening before.

Normally, in any interview situation, the Baron would come straight to the point. On this occasion, however, he seemed reluctant to.

'These quarters are to your liking?' he asked, casually prodding the stonework with his boot.

'They are more than adequate, sir, yes thank you.'

'A trifle chilly perhaps? When the wind is in the north?'

'My duties rarely allow me the comforts of the castle for a sustained period, sir. When I am here, I am content with my lodgings.'

'I see,' nodded the Baron. An uncomfortable silence began to grow, and the Baron had no option but to broach the reason for his visit.

'You are unhappy that I allowed the prisoner to be released?'

Tache raised his eyebrows, uncertain of where Baron Hart was going with this question. 'I am a soldier, sir, my opinion of my orders is irrelevant.'

'A tactful answer, Tache, and a worthy one too. Nevertheless, your opinion is not irrelevant to me.'

'Well then, sir, I would confess that I had reservations about the advice you were given to release the prisoner.'

Baron Hart nodded vigorously in agreement. 'Quite so. It commends us all to be cautious. It is for that reason that I must order you from the castle once more.'

'Sir?'

'You will choose two good men, who you can trust with your life. The three of you will follow the covert officer you know as Mozz. He himself will be following the prisoner. It is absolutely imperative that you do not interfere with that, do you understand?'

'Yes, sir!' replied Tache, his interest clearly roused.

'Report to me by word of mouth only. Send your man directly to me. You must be ready to support Mozz if required, but you must also be alert for anything untoward. Am I making myself clear?'

'Yes, sir!'

'The rest of the company may stand down. There will be no searches, no checkpoints. I no longer wish the children arrested, unless at the direct command of the officer, Mozz. It is time to try new tactics.'

'Very well, sir. Just as you wish.'

The Baron held the gaze of his captain for several moments.

'You know of the prophecy, and its importance. Do not fail me.'

Captain Tache stood to attention and saluted.

'I will do my duty, sir!'

The Baron appeared to be about to say something else, but thinking better of it, merely nodded and walked briskly out of the door.

Captain Tache went to the window of his room and watched the Baron marching across the cobbled courtyard of the bailey, his slight limp apparent in his gait – in his day, the Baron had been a fighting man.

A flurry of autumn leaves, blown from one of the few trees that grew within the keep, danced madly around the Baron's feet as he walked. Captain Tache watched him cross the bailey and disappear through a studded oak door on the far side. Then he sat back with a sigh, and wondered, not for the first time, if the day would come when the Baron could surprise him no more.

The Wetlands

When Terry got back down into the ravine, he found that the snow was not particularly deep. Some drifting had occurred up against the larger boulders, but nothing substantial enough to cause any difficulties for their journey back. The ravine stood empty and silent in the shadow of the surrounding peaks. Although it retained a sombre air, the snow had managed to soften something of its harshness, emphasising the stillness all around. Weaving here and there across the pristine surface were numerous paw tracks – testament to the fact that, for some creature at least, the ravine was a home. Terry guessed that perhaps a hare, or something of the sort, had been out and about once the blizzard had abated. He wondered where, in such a bleak terrain, it might be hiding now, and perhaps watching as they prepared to leave.

The morsk stood and stamped their feet impatiently while they were re-saddled, keen to be underway. Snorting noisily, their moist breaths condensed in the frosty air, like steam from a boiling kettle. Normally, the creatures had a dull, somewhat morose look about them, but now there was a keen and lively interest in their bulging blood-shot eyes. Every now and then, they would throw back their heads and bray loudly.

'The morsk seem happier up here,' observed Terry as he rejoined the group.

'Because this is their natural home,' replied Gwen, smiling knowingly. 'Perhaps they can even catch the scent of their wild cousins, a little farther to the north.'

'Well it ain't *my* natural home,' said Clumber ruefully, cupping her hands around her mouth and blowing warm air onto her numb fingers. 'I can't hardly get these saddle buckles done up, 'cos o' the cold. I'll be glad to see one o' Herstan's fires again, back in the Anchor Tavern.'

'There is a lot of ground to cover before we can enjoy such comforts again,' said Gwen grimly.

When at last they were ready to leave, they paused and looked back up to the ledge high above them. There was no sign of Hellaine – only a solitary bird, gazing disdainfully down on them. Lowering their heads resignedly, they sat slumped in their saddles and began the long, slow descent back towards the Great Plain of Carthag.

Meeshka summed up their mood best of all when she said to nobody in particular 'I'm not sure how I feel.' Certainly, despite the cosiness of Hellaine's cave, they were glad to be leaving the desolate terrain for warmer climes. Every foot of descent lessened the grip of the icy snow that plastered the windward side of any exposed rock-face.

Somehow though, having found the Watcher as the clue had indicated, they had hoped to come away understanding more of what they were doing, and why.

'I know what you mean,' agreed Gwen, 'but it is not Hellaine's fault she could not tell us more. We will all feel better once we are safely back in Piree.'

'And then I will solve the new clue,' said Polka confidently. Terry looked across at Polka with a mixture of hope and interest. 'I hope it will be that easy,' he replied thoughtfully, 'because there will be another four to follow.'

They rode on in silence for a short distance, and then Terry said 'Hellaine told me something else, just as I was leaving.'

'What was it?' asked Meeshka.

'She heard Yalyf talking in his sleep. There is a letter that might be found, and if it is, some secret about Castle Turuk could be discovered.'

'That is interesting,' said Gwen seriously. 'Perhaps the castle is connected in some way to the seven stones.'

'I hope not' replied Terry earnestly. 'If that's where the Baron lives, I would prefer to stay as far away as possible.'

'Let's 'ope we get a choice,' said Clumber gravely.

'The other thing that's bothering me,' continued Terry, 'is what Hellaine said about these Sans-Schen things – the shadow people. Have you ever heard of them before, Gwen?'

'No, not at all. We must try and find out more about them.'

'Hellaine said they were worse than the Bandero,' said Meeshka nervously.

'And they just appear suddenly, and disappear,' added Polka.

'Yes, but what have they got to do with it all?' asked Terry. 'That's what I don't understand.'

'Well, at least we understand that we do not understand things yet,' replied Gwen, determined to be positive. 'And look now,' she continued brightly, 'already the snow's grip is lessening.'

As they descended, it seemed that the snow was indeed confined to the high passes of the mountains, just as Hellaine had predicted. Once they were out of the ravine, their passage eased considerably, and in under an hour they were riding through coarse, green pasture once again. By mid-day they were back at the fork in the river, where their campsite had been the night before last. Here they paused to discuss the best route home.

'We can't risk running into the slave traders again,' said Gwen. 'Even though it will take us out of our way, we must turn east now and stay amongst the foothills for some time.'

'That will add two days to the journey,' moaned Clumber. 'I am ready for a hot meal and a warm fire already.'

'I know that,' replied Gwen firmly, 'and you are not the only one. All the same, you, Clumber, more than any of us, should know how dangerous those people are. It is better to get home two days later, than not at all.'

'Will the provisions last out?' asked Meeshka.

'Comfortably, and with some to spare,' nodded Gwen. 'I had not calculated on being so well fed by Hellaine. We will make the best of it, and return a little late, but safe.' In her heart, Clumber knew that Gwen was right, and although she scowled miserably, she gave her no further argument.

So east they turned, rather that following the river south, and they stayed close to the mountains for the rest of the day. Mostly they kept to just below the ridge lines, gazing down precipitous slopes into valleys full of rich green conifers. At the very bottom of these valleys, where the trees were thinned back by the narrow flood plain, a fast flowing river would be glinting in the bright sunshine. Terry longed to stop and explore, enthralled by the spectacle of a true wilderness. What struck him most was the breath-taking silence all around them.

On the second day they turned south, and almost immediately the terrain began to soften. The crests becoming more rounded, the scree slopes less hectic in their descents. It was as if a giant roller had done its best to flatten out the landscape, but not quite succeeded. For three more days they journeyed south through the undulating foothills. The weather stayed cold but fine, with crystal clear blue sky most of the time. Twice, they had significant river crossings to make, but although fast-flowing, the water was shallow enough to present no serious problems. The morsk were sure-footed and entirely comfortable in the icy water. Only once did they encounter another living soul, and only then from a distance. It was towards the end of their third day in the foothills, when Clumber pointed out a lonely figure, camping by a stream on the opposite side of the valley they were in. Immediately they took cover behind some large boulders and discussed the situation.

'Did they see us?' asked Terry.

'Couldn't say for sure,' replied Clumber, peering cautiously over one of the rocks. 'They ain't doing much. Just startin' a fire, I reckon.'

'It could it be one of the slave-traders,' suggested Meeshka anxiously.

'Maybe,' acknowledged Gwen, 'they have no stock with them, so I do not think it is a shepherd.'

'Well they ain't gotta morsk either though,' pointed out Clumber, 'an' there's just the one of 'em.' They watched warily for several minutes, but either the lone traveller had not seen them, or had no interest in them. They did not want to stay where they were until nightfall, so eventually they decided to take the risk and show themselves. Emerging from behind the boulders, they traversed around the side of the valley until they were out of sight, and then Clumber crept back alone to see if they were followed. She returned after twenty minutes with re-assuring news.

'He ain't moved a jot. He's cooking summat on his fire. I don't reckon we need worry much over 'im, whoever he is.' Relieved, they moved on quickly, and made best use of the remaining daylight.

When they finally stopped to camp by a grassy hummock on the very edge of the foothills, they enjoyed a tremendous view south over the plain.

'Everything is turning to soup!' exclaimed Polka. The others smiled because they knew just what he meant. Below them, for as far as they could see, swirling autumn mists clung to the land. Here and there, the dark silhouettes of tall trees could be seen standing proud in an ever shifting sea of grey that filled the whole of the vast plain. Above this soft carpet of mist, a pair of ducks tracked hurriedly south, whilst higher still, the mares' tail cirrus clouds were tainted a rich pink by a sun that was already set.

'It is very beautiful,' warned Gwen, 'but soon it will be dark. We must post lookouts and have only a small well-shielded cooking fire.' A larger fire would have kept them warmer, but might have attracted unwelcome attention, so no-one ventured to argue. They pitched the two tents face to face for extra warmth, and passed a cold but uneventful night, huddled close together beneath their blankets. Although they were not disturbed, the night seemed full of strange unidentified sounds, and none of them slept well.

The next day they finally descended out of the foothills, and onto the Great Plain itself. The terrain was suddenly much easier, and under the midday sun it even felt quite warm again, lightening their mood considerably. They were moving into an area known as the Wetlands, so named because of the numerous small and invariably shallow lakes that were scattered randomly over the coarse pasture. Many of these lakes were transitory, disappearing completely in high summer. Through rainy seasons though, shorelines became treacherously variable, as the water ebbed and flowed over the flat and featureless landscape. This made navigating the area a difficult and most tedious affair.

'At least we are not likely to run into those slave traders around here,' Gwen had said with some satisfaction, despite the fact that for the umpteenth time that day, they were retracing their steps. Often they would come across a lake and choose to skirt either eastward or westward around it. Sometimes their choice was good, and they would find a route through to drier ground. Other times though, they would find that the lake had virtually merged with another, and the land between them was too boggy for the morsk to readily traverse without becoming exhausted. The only thing to do was to return to their starting point and try the opposite way around the lake.

'We'll never get home at this rate,' moaned Clumber, 'I don't never want to see another lake again.'

'It is most aggravating,' agreed Gwen, 'but there is nothing we can do about it. I think perhaps we should make camp early tonight, on the next bit of firm dry ground we find.'

'That sounds like a good idea,' agreed Terry, who was as frustrated as Clumber by their poor progress. 'Let's take a chance on a decent fire tonight. I know there is not much cover, but no-one else is mad enough to be within miles of this place.'

Casting caution to the wind, they did exactly that, all five of them roaming far and wide to gather all the tinder they could, and heaping it up onto a veritable bonfire. It did their spirits good to feel warm again, and even Clumber was satisfied. They had to sit a goodly distance from the fire, such was the power of its heat. The morsk did not share their delight, preferring to be tethered well away from the flames.

They had amassed enough tinder to keep a fine blaze going until dawn, so a pleasant night's sleep was guaranteed. Although both Gwen and Meeshka were nervous that the fire would be visible from many miles away, once again, the night passed without incident. Terry and Clumber were on the last watch, having relieved Gwen in the early hours, but in the warmth of the fire, they both succumbed to sleep long before dawn.

Terry woke with a start, realising he had been asleep on his watch. Clumber slept soundly beside him, her breathing deep and regular. The fire was a smouldering ruin, for it had not been tendered for a couple of hours. Terry shivered involuntarily, for there was a bitter chill in the dawn that penetrated deeply, now that the protection of the fire was removed. There was a grey half-light, and at first Terry thought that it must still be early. As he became fully awake though, he realised that the poor light was due to a thick and freezing fog that must have descended under cover of darkness. It was unusually dense, making it impossible to see more than five or six metres in any direction.

He woke the others, and then rekindled the fire in order for them to cook some breakfast. Over their meal, they debated the best course of action. Clumber was for pressing on, regardless of the fog. 'It'll prob'ly just clear anyhows,' she argued, 'once the sun gets up a bit.'

'Well without the sun to guide us, we would be lost in minutes,' replied Gwen, 'unless one of you has a compass.' Nobody did, so there was nothing to do but sit it out by the fire, each of them growing more impatient to be under way.

After an hour or so, with the remaining tinder used up and the fire dying back down, Clumber suggested that they at least saddle up the morsk and get ready to leave as soon as the fog showed any sign of lifting. This seemed a sensible suggestion, and gave them something positive to do, rather than simply sitting and getting cold. Before long they were standing by their saddled morsk, anxiously watching for any change in conditions. And it seemed that their luck was in, for after only a short wait, Clumber suddenly yelled triumphantly, 'Look! The sun is breaking through!' Above them, the sun's disc could indeed be seen, although it lacked any power and their eyes could tolerate staring directly towards it. Then it was gone, but then back again, and stronger. Looking around, they could now see a decent distance – perhaps twenty metres or more, and their hopes were raised.

'I do believe we can make a start,' said Gwen cautiously.

'O' course we can,' snorted Clumber impatiently, digging her heels into the side of her morsk.

'Be careful though,' warned Terry. 'Keep together.'

Clumber led them off in single file, while Terry dropped to the rear. Gwen followed Clumber, and then Meeshka. 'Stay close behind me Polka,' Meeshka advised her brother, 'I do not like the look of this.'

They made slow but steady progress, all the time hoping that the fog would lift completely. Frustratingly though, it clung stubbornly to the land, sometimes thinning encouragingly, but then returning suddenly and unexpectedly. It never quite lifted enough for them to gain a good perspective on where they were, so they could only keep heading vaguely south and trust that they were not going too far astray. Around mid-afternoon, the fog became extremely dense once more, and they were forced to stop. Straight away, it was clear that something was wrong.

'Look at the morsk,' wailed Meeshka anxiously. The beast shuffled nervously, and an oily sweat gleamed on their coats, even though they had not been unduly exerted. They each had a wild look in their eyes.

'What is wrong with them?' asked Terry, mystified by their behaviour. 'Is it just the fog that's upsetting them?'

'I don't think so,' replied Gwen, 'it didn't bother them before.'

'Well something has spooked them, that's for sure,' said Terry.

Suddenly, Clumber's morsk reared high on its hind legs, nearly throwing her clear.

'Whoa there!' she cried in alarm, and it took all her skill to stay in the saddle. Another morsk then kicked savagely backwards, just missing the flank of Polka's animal.

'Stay calm,' cried Gwen desperately, as panic spread amongst the animals, but it was hopeless. Meeshka's morsk reared alarmingly, and then set off at full gallop into the fog, which had closed in even more densely around them. 'Meeshka!' yelled Gwen, just as her own creature did exactly the same. Then Terry too found that he was sitting astride a powerful animal that was galloping blindly and recklessly into an unknown oblivion. No matter how he tried to rein it back by tugging forcefully on the antlers, there was no stopping it. He heard cries of dismay from Clumber and Polka behind him, and then a silence, punctuated only by the frantic hoof beats of his mount. The icy slipstream of the fog stung his face, but all he could do was wait for the beast to tire, or tumble. If it were the latter, he knew his own prospects were fairly grim. Then suddenly there was water everywhere. His morsk was skittering through the shallows of one of the numerous lakes. The spray flew high into the air under the force of the gallop, splattering Terry from above and below. At last though, there was some lessening of the morsk's pace as its confusion began to replace panic. It trod a wide circle, slowing all the time, and eventually it came to a shuddering halt, snorting loudly, its breathing deep and rapid.

'Coosh now,' murmured Terry, softly stroking the creature's neck. He dismounted, standing beside the creature in the freezing water, and gently comforting it until its breathing returned to normal. The fog was still dense, and he could no longer see the shore of the lake, but at least the water only came up to his knees. When the morsk seemed calm enough, he made an estimate of the direction they had come from, and tried to retrace their steps. He coaxed the animal through the gently lapping waters, and to his relief, the boggy shoreline soon appeared again. He led the animal onto slightly higher ground, and watched amazed as it began to graze unconcernedly, as if nothing untoward had taken place.

Terry stood listening for any sound in the fog. Then he called the others, in measured tones at first, but when he got no reply, at the top of his voice. There was only silence – a grim, grey, damp silence. Using the halter, he led the morsk on foot, back the way he thought they had come. With no feature to guide him, the route he took was nothing more than guesswork. After a few minutes, he stopped, sure that he could hear voices. They were very muffled, and he could not make out for certain what was being said. He called, then yelled, but again there was no reply. Then he heard something more clearly. Although distant and strangely distorted by the fog, it was definitely Meeshka, her voice raised in fear and alarm.

'It's over there! Look out! Look out! It's coming back!'

And then another voice – surely it must have been Gwen?

'Wait there, I'm coming!'

Frantically, Terry called out. 'Meeshka! Gwen! What's happening? Where are you?' He waited, listening, and then called again. And then again, but they did not answer. For half an hour, he stood rooted to the spot, dividing his time between calling and listening, but he did not hear their voices again, nor any other sound of note. He had no idea what trouble his friends had been facing, nor how they had fared against it.

Although it was difficult to be sure, Terry sensed that the light was lessening, and guessed that darkness was not far away. Still the fog lingered, dense as ever, so that he stood in an isolated patch of lichen and heather, not able to see more than a few metres. His morsk waited patiently beside him, gazing morosely into the impenetrable mist. Terry tightened his grip on the collar lead, for he knew that his very survival depended now on his morsk. The temperature would drop close to freezing in the night, and there was little cover to be found. He knew his saddlebag held neither tent nor tinderbox, so there would be no shelter and no fire. Terry had been well coached in outdoor ways, and he knew enough about the dangers of exposure and hypothermia to understand that with little to protect him, his life was in danger. His only chance was to find as dry and sheltered a place as he could, and if it would allow him, spend the night by his morsk, using its precious body heat to maintain his own. With little light left to find a suitable spot to spend the night, he began his search without delay. He was fortunate in that he quickly found a small rocky gully, cut into a small rise by a stream that had since dried up. He led the morsk as far into the cut as it would allow, and then tethered it firmly to a protruding rock. He would have preferred to have been a little deeper into the gully, but once the morsk had decided it would go no further, any continued effort was futile. Examining his saddlebag, he discovered that he had spare clothes, and a little food, both of which would help. Nevertheless, it was going to be a long and uncomfortable night. Worse still, it would be spent in total ignorance of what fate had befallen his friends.

Lost in the Fog

When Clumber's morsk bolted, she was already expecting it. Having been riding from the age of four, she possessed both experience and natural talent. The combination of these two assets gave her the necessary means to deal with the situation. Although of slender build, her wiry frame actually packed surprising strength, which was a third and decisive factor. She allowed the morsk sufficient time to get over its initial wave of panic, and establish itself into a steady gallop. Then she pushed down viciously on the animal's right antler, pressing as far as she could reach, until the tip of the antler was almost touching the top of her boot. This action caused the morsk's head to be twisted at such an obtuse and painful angle, that it was impossible for it to maintain the gallop. It came to a rapid shuddering halt, and Clumber held it there. She quickly dismounted, whilst still holding the animal's right antler down towards the stirrups. Then she made a successful grab for the precious neck halter. The beast was clearly not happy with the situation, and it stamped and brayed loudly whilst kicking out savagely to the rear. Clumber was too well-versed in the ways of morsk to be caught out by such tactics, and she held her grip firmly until the kicks and stamping subsided. Then gradually, she began to relax her pressure a little. Unfortunately, there was absolutely no warning whatsoever when Polka's morsk came thundering out of the dense fog behind her at full gallop. It thudded into the rear flank of her own morsk, lifting its hind legs clear of the ground and spinning it through a quarter turn. Despite everything, Clumber managed to keep hold of the halter, although in so doing, her shoulder was given a painful jolt.

Polka fared less well. The front legs of his morsk buckled on impact, and he was thrown clean off his saddle and over its head. His chest caught the rump of Clumber's morsk, which took much of the momentum out of his flight. Although this was painful enough in itself, it probably saved him from serious injury, and possibly saved his life. He fell to the ground on the far side of the two morsk, and rolled over twice. His shoulder grazed a large stone, but his head came into contact only with the soft and boggy ground. Severely winded, and with his shoulder stinging as if it had been scalded, he slowly sat up and looked around in confusion. Then, covered in mud, he shakily stood up. Directly in front of him, the two morsk seemed to recover at the same instant, and clambered hurriedly to their feet. The shock and pain of what had happened had dispelled all sense of their previous panic. They simply stood there silently with their heads lowered, looking very sorry for themselves.

'Are you OK?' asked Clumber anxiously. 'Yer didn't 'alf whack into that morsk.' Polka blinked and stared ahead vacantly, unsure for a moment what had happened. As Clumber's question filtered slowly into his mind, he began to recover.

'I think I am,' he gasped, 'but my shoulder hurts a lot.'

'Mine too,' said Clumber, ruefully rubbing her own injury. 'At least the morsk seem OK. You better get a hold of yours in case it tries to do a runner again.' Polka took the halter of his animal and gave it a reassuring pat.

'What should we do now?' he asked.

'Try an' find the others again, I 'spose,' replied Clumber with a shrug.

'Everyone's morsk charged off.'

'I know, I'll try givin' them a shout.' Clumber put her considerable vocal talents to good use, but after several minutes even she was hoarse, and there had been no reply.

'It's no good,' she gasped, 'this 'ere fog just kills any sound.'

'Maybe we just try and find our way back to where we were,' suggested Polka. 'That's probably what the others will do.'

'Makes sense,' agreed Clumber. They did their best to retrace their steps, but the fog was so dense, it was impossible to recognise the way they had come. One piece of boggy turf looked pretty much like another when you couldn't see more than a few metres. After wandering uncertainly for some time, Clumber began to get suspicious that they were off track. When they came to the gently lapping edge of yet another shallow lake, they both knew it for sure.

'It ain't no good,' said Clumber gloomily, 'we'll never find that spot again. Even if we did, the others won't. We might as well just stick about an' 'ope that this fog'll lift.'

They led their morsk along the shoreline of the lake, hoping to find a better place to sit out the fog. After a short distance, they came to some raised ground, strewn with several large boulders. Clambering up amongst the rocks, they found a dry sheltered hollow filled with heather. The morsk seemed to catch on that they were going no further for the time being, and quickly settled down side by side. Clumber and Polka squeezed in between them where, for a cold and foggy day out in the open, it was as cosy as it was going to get.

'Maybe we could solve the next clue while we're waiting,' said Polka philosophically.

''Cept that we ain't got it,' replied Clumber gloomily. 'Terry's got it.'

'I can remember it.'

Clumber looked at Polka in genuine surprise. 'I know there was summat about NEW SNOW, but I'd never remember it exactly.'

'It was NEW 7, SNOW 11, HERE 23.'

'Well, I reckon that sounds right, but it makes no sense to me.'

'The key to it is understanding why the numbers are there. Suppose 7 meant the seventh letter of the alphabet, and so on.'

Clumber shifted uncomfortably. 'I ain't so good with letters and the like,' she admitted coyly. 'Herstan an' Freda 'ave done their best by me, but I don't seem to 'ave much talent for it.'

'Don't worry,' said Polka generously. 'You're good at other things, like controlling mad morsk.' Clumber blushed modestly, and was about to say something when Polka suddenly gripped her arm tightly.

'Sshh!' he said softly, 'I think I can hear voices.' They both listened intently for a while. At first there was nothing, but just when Polka was starting to think he had imagined it, they heard the unmistakeable sound of men's voices, and they seemed to be quite close now. The two of them crept carefully out from between the morsk to avoid disturbing them, and then shuffled on their bellies to the rim of the hollow they were lying in. Cautiously, they peeped over the edge, and got a considerable shock. The fog must have played its trick with the sound again, because standing just five metres below them, holding the halters of their morsk, were four men. Although one had his back to them, Polka immediately recognised the walnut coloured bald head of Mozz. The other three were clearly Bandero officers. As the children listened, an argument was developing.

'Curse this fog,' growled Captain Tache. 'The plan has failed. The boatman has led us on a fool's trail, from Carthag to this loathsome place, and never a sign of his wife or the children.'

'Be patient, Tache,' replied Mozz calmly. 'I know this boatman, and he is artful. No doubt he expected to be followed, and has behaved accordingly. But he must show his hand in time.'

'We should arrest him now, before we lose him in this fog,' persisted the Captain.

'No. He is pinned down like the rest of us for the time being. We know where he is camped, and he will be there until the fog lifts.'

'And then what?'

'And then we shall see.'

'You told the Baron that the prisoner would lead us to the child, and thus to the stones. He has not done so. We must arrest him again.'

'You will not arrest him, Tache,' replied Mozz angrily. 'I was not present at the time you received your orders, but we both know what they were. You have taken a risk in this rendezvous, even allowing for the cover of the fog. You will return to your station and await my signal, and that is the end of the matter.' Mozz turned sharply on his heels and lead his morsk away into the fog. The three Bandero stood there sullenly, and then Captain Tache picked up a small rock and hurled it savagely at the small hill. Clumber and Polka ducked instinctively as it smashed into the lip of the hollow. It sent several smaller bits of earth splattering into the depression, landing on the two morsk sheltering there. For one awful second, Clumber and Polka thought they were going to rise, but they merely shifted their legs awkwardly and widened their bloodshot eyes in alarm. By the time Clumber and Polka next dared look over the rim, the Bandero had disappeared.

'Who the 'eck was that?' asked Clumber.

'That was Mozz,' replied Polka grimly. 'He is a traitor.'

Scattered

If Terry slept at all during the long night, he was not aware that he had. The morsk had settled itself after an hour or so, and seemed indifferent when he gingerly lay down beside it. With both sharp antlers and sharp hooves to be avoided, it was difficult for him to find a position where he would benefit from the animal's body warmth, but he managed as best he could, propped up against its back. He was disappointed at how little heat escaped through the creature's thick hide, and the remorseless cold seeped through his body as the night progressed, making it an uncomfortable and lengthy vigil. He spent the most part of it rubbing his arms and legs to try to keep some warmth within them. And when he was not doing that, he was thinking.

Perhaps for the first time since he had come to Gwen's

World (as he was now calling it, to himself at least) he reviewed in his mind all that had happened. There was so much he didn't understand. Starting with the moment he had entered the Huntsman's Cottage in Crow Wood – who had left the footprints, and placed the first stone on the mantelpiece? And what was the torus? How did it move you between worlds? He had left his own world in late spring, yet arrived here in the autumn. Perhaps that meant that Carthag was in the southern hemisphere of Gwen's world, and yet it couldn't be – the stars here were the familiar stars of the northern hemisphere. If the different worlds were all just different futures of the same world, as Hellaine had suggested, then how could this make sense? Central to the mystery of what was happening to him was Yalyf – if he could only work out who Yalyf was – then perhaps, he would be able to understand the significance of the seven stones. Why were these stones so important, and why had he been chosen to find them? At some time in the future, would everything fit together and make sense? At the moment, he felt like he was seeing just a few pieces of a giant jigsaw. It was impossible to fit them together and reveal the hidden picture.

The cold dark night gave him only the time in which to think – it held no answers to his many questions. He spent an hour or so trying to solve the new clue, but could make no progress with it. As the night drew on, determination gave way to frustration, and frustration to depression. There was one moment, an hour or so before dawn, when his spirits were lifted a little, as he suddenly became aware that the blackness above him was full of stars. Their silent emergence, on mass, bore witness to the fact that the fog had lifted at last, giving him much needed hope for the new dawn.

The morsk stirred before Terry. Snorting loudly, it woke with a start and clambered suddenly to its feet in an ungainly manner. Terry then found himself lying in a dangerous position beneath it, so he very quickly rose as well, stamping his feet and rubbing the palms of his hands together to try and dispel the numbness which had crept into them during the night. He led the morsk out of the narrow gully, and was then able to see that the eastern horizon had a band of turquoise light above it. The night had been unpleasant, but he had survived it.

Rummaging in his saddlebag, he found a piece of fruitcake that he had overlooked the previous evening, and this constituted his breakfast, for now at least. It tasted so much better than fruitcake had ever tasted before. After completing his frugal meal, he considered his options. It occurred to him that before it became fully light, he should climb to the top of the small rise through which the gully was cut. It was too small to be called a hill, but given that all of the surrounding terrain was predominantly flat, it would offer a good vantage point from which to take bearings. He tethered the morsk loosely to a boulder, allowing it to graze contentedly. He would have liked to have offered it some bran, but he knew that what little they had was in Polka's saddlebag. Then he climbed the short distance to the top of the rise and surveyed the surrounding land. He was careful not to rush – starting from the north, he considered small sectors in turn, scrutinising the semi-darkness for any signs of life. And his patience was rewarded, for to the south-west, he saw just what his eyes were seeking – the flickering light of a small campfire.

Although the temptation to set out immediately was very strong, Terry was able to resist it, for two reasons.

Firstly, he could not yet see far enough in the darkness to be able to take reliable long distance bearings. He marked the direction with nearby objects, but he knew that once he had set off, if the fire were to be extinguished, he would be left to guesswork. If he had to skirt around a lake, he would have no chance of getting back on track. The sun would be up well before he reached the fire, and the campsite would be very easy to miss if he lost the line of its direction. His second reason for delaying was to give his morsk time to graze – he expected he would be demanding another day's hard riding from the creature, and he already considered he owed it much.

As soon as the first shaft of sunlight pierced the horizon, Terry set off towards where he had seen the fire. He now had several waypoints in both the middle and far distance, by which to judge the direction he should take. It was still early, and if the fire had belonged to his friends, he was confident they would not have moved on before he arrived. He was resolved to be careful, however, and long before he reached the spot where he judged the fire to have been, he dismounted and led his morsk on foot. There had been no lakes to navigate around, but the area was quite boggy still. Tufts of coarse grass grew to waist height in places, swaying under the bitterly cold breeze that blew down from the north. Although Terry knew he had this to thank for removing the fog, still he could not welcome it.

He noticed a thin wisp of smoke from about two hundred metres, rising almost exactly from the point where his precise navigation had suggested the fire would have been. He tethered his morsk and approached with extreme caution. There was some undulation to the terrain that allowed him partial cover, but nevertheless, if lookouts were posted, his approach could not have gone unnoticed. As he got closer, he got down on his belly and crawled through the grass towards the camp. From twenty metres, he could see that the camp was now deserted, so throwing caution to the wind, he rose up and walked boldly up to the smouldering ashes of the fire. It had been built in a circle of small stones, and these were still warm to the touch. He examined the camp carefully, trying to decide if it had been made by any of his friends.

'Good day to you, youngster. I am most surprised to see you again.'

Terry whirled around in alarm, to find Mozz sitting in the grass, watching him with a quizzical grin.

'If you hoped to surprise the Bandero, whose fire this was,' Mozz continued, 'then you were incautious. I saw you from five minutes away, and heard you from two. They would have lured you into a trap.'

Terry hesitated for a moment before replying, taking in the meaning of what Mozz was saying. 'I did not know this camp was made by Bandero,' he said at last. 'I had hoped it was made by my friends. I have lost contact with them.'

This time, it was Mozz who waited before replying. He regarded Terry carefully, gleaning what information he could with his eyes before resorting to questions.

'You look as if you have had a difficult night in the open, youngster. You had better sit down and tell me what you are doing here, so far out on the plain, and how you have become separated from your friends.'

Terry thought back to the night they had evaded the Bandero at the canal junction. If Mozz had wanted to betray them, it would have been easy for him to have done so then. In any case, it was Mozz who had given him the encouraging message from Yalyf, suggesting they should find the one who knew they were coming, which could only have meant the Watcher. Terry felt confident he could trust Mozz, but he was also conscious of the warning in the first riddle – *trust in few*.

'I need to think a moment,' he said hesitantly. Mozz looked at him keenly, and then nodded slowly. 'Take your time, youngster. You can tell me all or naught. Either way, you will come to no harm from me.'

Terry thought long and hard. He knew he would have to choose his words carefully. When at last he reached his decision, he felt more comfortable.

'If you don't mind,' he began apologetically, 'there are some things I would prefer not to say until I am certain I can trust you.'

'Very wise,' replied Mozz encouragingly.

'But I will tell you the main things that have happened since I last met you.'

Mozz nodded once more, and gestured for them both to sit down.

'We have been to see someone called the Watcher,' continued Terry, once he was comfortable, 'in a ravine, up in the mountains. We think she was the one your message refers to – the one who knew we were coming. She spent a lot of time with Yalyf, the one you call the Stranger, when he was here a long time ago. She has explained to us that we need to find some stones that were left by him. We don't know why it is important to do this, but something bad could happen if we don't. Also, I cannot go home until I have found all the stones. While we were staying with the Watcher, we discovered a clue to help us find these stones, but we have not been able to solve it yet. We still do not know who Yalyf was, or why he left the stones, or what happened to him. On our way back we got separated in the fog, and that's why I'm here on my own. That's about it really.'

When he had finished, Mozz smiled knowingly. 'A good account, youngster. Not quite complete, as you forewarned me, but that is to your credit. You will recall I warned you myself to be careful who you trust.'

Terry looked up into the piercing blue eyes of the boatman, and felt very vulnerable. He was conscious of the two stones hidden in the secret pocket of his waistcoat, but he tried not to think about them. 'If I may,' he said boldly, 'I have some questions of my own.'

Mozz grinned, almost to himself, and then said loftily 'Ask away.'

Terry hardly knew where to start, but the mention of the Bandero seemed the most pressing concern. 'Are the Bandero following me?' he began.

Mozz had not been promoted to the Baron's covert elite without good reason – he thought well on his feet. Terry had surprised him completely, but already he was plotting how to make gains from the situation. Knowing that Captain Tache and his men were several miles south, he nevertheless had decided straight away to pretend that the fire was theirs. He reasoned that Terry was more likely to enlist his help if the Bandero were thought to be an immediate threat. In fact, the fire had been Hev's, and Terry had missed being re-united with him by only a matter of twenty minutes. Mozz also knew that the finest strategies need an element of luck. As a professional soldier, he had learnt to accept what came his way, and adjust his plans accordingly. If he played his cards carefully, he could use this opportunity to gain the boy's trust completely. All of this, he had considered in an instant, and determined his course of action.

'No,' he replied without hesitation, 'they are following me – but, doubtless in the hope that I will lead them to you.'

'So, are *you* following me?'

'No, again. As I told you, I am most surprised to see you here.'

'Have you seen Gwen and the others?'

'No, a third time, but have no fear. I am sure they will not be far away. We must hope they do not have the misfortune to encounter the Bandero.'

'So what *are* you doing here, Mozz?'

'I first travelled north, seeking you, but I was followed by the Bandero. I did not want to lead them to you, so I turned east into the Wetlands, to try and lose them. Since then, we have played a cat and mouse game. The fog has finally given me the chance to throw them off my trail, or so I hope.'

'Why are you seeking me now, when back at the canal you were happy just to give me your message and leave me to my fate?'

'A fair question,' nodded Mozz, 'and one I have posed to myself, more than once of late. Since that night, youngster, I have had time to reflect on matters. The stranger we knew as Yalyf, I was proud to call my friend. In the short time I knew him, he taught me much about myself. In the end, I could not consider my debt paid to him by just passing on my message to you. These are dangerous times, and there are desperate people around, who have an interest in the legend of the stones. You are not native to these parts, and will need what protection you can find if you are to succeed in your quest. I am here only to offer my help, for I know now that my heart will allow me no peace if I do not see this through with you.'

'But why are the Bandero following you?'

'Another good question. I can only conclude that they are better informed than I imagined. Someone has perhaps mentioned my association with the stranger, many years ago. Now that you have come at last, the Bandero have thought it wise to keep watch on me, just in case. Baron Hart is a formidable and resourceful foe – for both of us, it would seem.'

'I see,' said Terry after a long pause. 'So what now? Could you help me find my friends?'

'Gladly, though it will not be difficult – look yonder!'

Terry followed Mozz's pointing arm to the west. He immediately saw a rising column of thick smoke, angled by the breeze, only two or three miles distant.

'We had better hurry,' advised Mozz. 'It is possible that such an incautious fire will not escape the attention of the Bandero.'

Mozz retrieved his morsk, cleverly tethered out of sight a short distance away, and they then retraced Terry's approach to where his own morsk was tethered.

'Speed is of the essence,' said Mozz grimly. 'We ride hard.'

Together, they urged their morsk into a gallop, heading straight for the rising smoke.

In the Company
of Traitors

Gwen and Meeshka had made a big fire, with the sole purpose of signalling their position to Terry, Polka and Clumber. Amongst the contents of their saddlebags had been one of the tents, most of the blankets, and the tinderbox. As a result, the two of them had passed a fairly comfortable night, their only distress being the absence of the others.

They had risen at dawn, and found themselves to the north of yet another large and shallow lake. Suitable tinder was scarce on the shoreline, and it had taken them a considerable time, exploring both east and west, to gather sufficient for a big blaze. Once they got the fire started though, they had placed enough greenery on it to make a good thick column of smoke. They both then stood and waited, watching the fire with a mixture of hope and anxiety. Their signal would be seen for miles, and would be seen by anyone in the area, friend or foe.

Clumber and Polka were the first to arrive, within a few minutes of the fire being lit. The fog had not given them the opportunity to move any further the previous afternoon, following their encounter with Mozz and the Bandero. Luckily for them, the other tent was in Clumber's saddlebag, and they had pitched it in the hollow basin of the raised ground. There they had spent a miserable night, sharing a single blanket. Even though they had most of the provisions with them, they were in no mood to feast, knowing that the others would be going hungry. Had they but known it, they had spent the night not five-hundred metres from Gwen and Meeshka. When dawn broke, Clumber had reasoned that it made sense to stay on the raised ground for a while, giving them a good vantage point to watch for both their friends, and the Bandero. They had been astonished to see a column of smoke so very close to their own camp. Approaching carefully, leading their morsk by hand, they were delighted to discover Gwen and Meeshka, busily heaping more fuel on the fire.

'We have seen the Bandero!' yelled Polka excitedly as they came into the camp. Fending off Meeshka's hug of welcome in his desire to impart the important news, he continued in urgent tones. 'The man, Mozz, was with them. He is a liar and a traitor! We overheard everything.'

'Come and have some breakfast,' said Gwen warmly, 'and tell us all you know.' Meeshka gave Clumber a hug too, quietly thanking her for looking after Polka. Clumber blushed scarlet at this attention, but seemed pleased.

'You must listen to me about the man, Mozz,' persisted

Polka. 'They are using Hev to try and find us. They know about the stones.'

'Hev was with them?' asked Gwen quickly, hope surging in her heart.

'No, but he has been released. They have been following him, hoping that he would lead them to the rest of us. He is camped somewhere near to here.'

'It's true, right 'nuff,' confirmed Clumber. 'That Mozz, 'e's a villain. Working for the Baron, all this time. We gotta warn Terry.'

'We need to *find* Terry first,' replied Gwen anxiously, 'but now I am worried that the Bandero will see this smoke. Perhaps we should put the fire out.' As they pondered this difficult decision, Polka made the debate irrelevant. He was crouching with his palm on the ground, gazing into the distance. 'People come,' he said soberly. 'Two riders, from the south.'

There was no time to do anything, not that there was anything they could have done. With growing tension, they simply stood and waited. Gwen placed a protective arm around Meeshka's shoulders, but nobody spoke as the two riders drew nearer. Then Polka ventured an opinion. 'I think one of them might be Terry,' he said quietly. Moments later, Clumber's keen eyesight confirmed this. 'It *is* Terry,' she said grimly, 'but the other one is Mozz.' They considered this unwelcome news in silence for a moment. Then Meeshka asked uneasily 'Gwen, what should we do?'

'Say nothing,' cautioned Gwen. 'Do not let Mozz know that we know he is a traitor. Otherwise he will fetch the Bandero, and we will all be arrested.' Mozz and Terry were almost upon them, and Gwen raised her arm to wave. 'Be pleased to see Terry,' she whispered frantically. 'Remember that he does not know about Mozz. We must all put on a good act.' She could say no more, because Terry was already jumping happily out of his saddle. Gwen ran towards him and gave him a hug. 'Oh Terry, I am so pleased to see you again,' she said in genuine relief. Then the others crowded around smiling, and Meeshka shyly patted Terry on the back. 'We have been worried about you,' she said quietly.

'I was worried about you too,' he replied. 'I heard you shouting in the fog. Something about *it's over there* and *lookout, it's coming back.*'

'Oh yes,' said Gwen, 'it was a kuru.'

'They are quite like bears,' explained Meeshka. 'We think that is why the morsk were panicked. They must have picked up its scent.'

'Were you OK?'

'Yes, Gwen threw a large stone and hit it on the head. It was a great shot. The kuru ran away.'

'It was a lucky shot,' said Gwen modestly. 'They can be very dangerous, but fortunately it was quite a young one.'

'Didn't you hear me calling you?' asked Terry. 'I shouted for ages.'

'We didn't hear anything,' replied Meeshka apologetically.

'That is often the way of things, in a fog such as that,' said Mozz, climbing down from his morsk. 'The sound will travel well enough in one direction, yet not at all in the other.'

'You remember Mozz,' said Terry by way of introduction. 'He was our towman for a while on the boat. And he told me how we needed to find someone who knew we were coming.'

Mozz nodded politely to them all, and looked curiously at Clumber.

'Me name's Clumber,' she said, but rather stiffly.

'Clumber is the niece of some friends of mine,' said Gwen rather hurriedly. She was anxious that Mozz did not learn any details that would link them to Herstan and Freda.

'Well met to you all then' said Mozz affably, and nodded once more to them.

'Mozz met Yalyf, years ago,' continued Terry enthusiastically, 'and he is going to help us. He came looking for us, but the Bandero have been following him. I have told him that we are trying to find the seven stones.' Clumber and Polka could not help exchanging ominous glances at this.

'I will do what I can to help,' confirmed Mozz. 'I feel I owe that to the stranger, Yalyf, who I was proud to call my friend for a while. I understand you have a clue to solve – have you had any luck with it?'

'No,' said Polka, rather too quickly, and Terry gave him a puzzled glance.

'Perhaps we will get a chance later,' said Gwen smoothly. 'For now, I suggest we all eat breakfast.'

'Not 'til we get this fire out,' said Clumber firmly, giving the fire a hefty kick to scatter the blaze. 'It's done its job, I reckon. We don't want the Bandero fetched 'ere an' all.' Polka helped her stamp out the remaining flames, and the breeze soon dispelled the last of the smoke. Gwen turned quickly to Mozz. 'You say the Bandero are following you?' she said, anxious to deflect any suggestion that Clumber already knew they were close by.

'Ever since Carthag,' answered Mozz. 'I have eluded them for the time being, but they may pick up my trail again shortly – and now yours too. Worse still, the trail will be easy to follow, on sodden ground such as this. I suggest we make haste with any breakfast, and break camp without delay.'

'But where should we head to?' asked Terry. 'Until we solve the next clue, we don't know where to go.'

'The *next* clue?' queried Mozz with interest. 'There have been others, then?'

'Well,' said Terry awkwardly, 'one other..., it was given to me at the beginning..., it told me to find the Watcher.'

A difficult silence followed. 'I have not told Mozz everything,' explained Terry to his friends. 'Not yet.'

'And I have told him that he is wise to be cautious,' said Mozz heartily, 'but perhaps I can be of *more* help if I understand more.' Again, there was a tense silence.

'I would like to talk to Terry about the next clue,' said Polka suddenly. 'I have an idea about it and I would like to tell Terry first.'

'That is a good idea Polka,' replied Gwen briskly. 'You two go and discuss it, and we will get breakfast ready as quickly as possible.' Terry looked very confused, but he allowed himself to be tugged away by Polka, and the others busied themselves getting the food ready. Mozz said nothing, but he could not completely hide the suspicion burning in his eyes. He sat down alone, and waited.

Polka and Terry were gone some time, and the others had begun their breakfast by the time they returned. Terry looked thoughtful, but he smiled confidently at Mozz as he sat down to his breakfast of gallash. 'How long before the Bandero pick up your trail again?' he asked airily.

'Not easy to say, youngster,' replied Mozz, his piercing blue eyes trying to read Terry's mood. 'It could be as much as a day, or as little as two hours.'

'So,' replied Terry, 'we need to leave here as soon as possible, just in case.'

'I believe we should,' agreed Mozz, 'but have you discovered where we need to go to find the stones?'

'Not yet, but we need to get out of these wetlands. The first priority is to lose the Bandero.'

'And how do you propose to do that?' asked Mozz with interest.

'We ride into the lake,' said Terry simply. Both Gwen and Meeshka cast anxious glances in Terry's direction, but he continued enthusiastically. 'The lakes are shallow. My morsk bolted into one yesterday, in the fog. It was probably smaller than this one, but even quite far out it only came up to my knees.'

'We cannot remain in the lake,' said Mozz dubiously.

'No, but we will try to find a rocky area by which to leave, concealing the trail. Then we will ride west, towards harder ground. We may not lose the Bandero completely, but it will hopefully delay them.'

'That's a good plan,' said Clumber eagerly. 'I reckon we oughta leave on the eastern shore, if we can — they ain't gonna expect us to be heading deeper into the Wetlands.'

'Good idea,' agreed Terry. Mozz seemed somewhat troubled by this plan, but he said nothing to dissuade them. Terry and Polka hurriedly ate their breakfast, while the others packed up the camp. Mozz remounted his own morsk and waited, glancing frequently at Terry with a thoughtful expression. When they were all ready, Terry led them over to the lake shore. 'Follow me,' he said confidently.

As expected, the lake proved to be very shallow, the water not even reaching the hock joints on the legs of their morsk. The bed of the lake was firm enough to cause no difficulties, and they waded some considerable distance from the shore before turning east. As they approached the eastern fringes, they made a very welcome discovery. A wide but shallow overspill flowed down into the lake from a further lake, some three hundred metres away. It was only a few centimetres deep, and clearly a temporary feature as there was no bed to it. The water was simply flowing over the grass. Terry led them up it, and their tracks were immediately erased within moments. Following its course into the second lake, they then searched the south-east corner for an appropriate place to come ashore. They found a wide bed of shingles, stretching for some distance along the shoreline, that was ideal. Each choosing different points to exit, they dismounted and led their morsk carefully over the stones, doing their best to leave no obvious signs. Terry noted with annoyance that Mozz did not take the same degree of care as the rest of them. They were all separated by thirty metres or so, but Terry moved straight over towards Gwen when they came off the shingle. He was able to snatch a very quick and whispered conversation.

'Polka has told me about Mozz, and that Hev is free. I haven't told Mozz that we have two stones already. If he knew, he would try to steal them. Try to warn the others not to mention it.'

'What are we going to do?' she whispered back urgently.

'We will try to lose him tonight. Polka has a plan. But Gwen...'

'What's wrong?'

'I told Mozz about the Watcher. I think I have put Hellaine in danger.'

'Maybe not. It is the stones they are after. In any case, Hellaine can take care of herself. Winter comes, and the Bandero will not find the ravine a hospitable place.'

There was no further chance to talk, as Mozz was rapidly approaching with the others.

'Do you think that will fool the Bandero?' Terry asked him innocently as he re-joined them.

'Well, I would not like to have to follow that trail myself,' replied Mozz, as he remounted his morsk. 'It would surely tax the skills of an expert tracker.'

'Let's hope so,' said Terry grimly. 'Now we must ride west, as fast as we can.'

'West, you say?' queried Mozz, but Terry had already kicked his morsk into a canter, and he did not reply.

At sunset, they stopped to make camp in the shadow of a small hill. A pleasant stream tumbled down its eastern flank, and alder trees lined the grassy banks. For the last two hours, they had been traversing ground that was both firmer and more undulating. The Wetlands were behind them at last.

'Where are we, would you say, Mozz?' asked Terry, as they unsaddled the morsk and set them on long tethers.

'I would judge we are due east of Piree,' he replied, after some reflection. 'One day's ride at a good gallop, maybe less. Is Piree our destination?'

'We are running short on provisions. We need to head there first, and re-stock. Then, when we understand what the clue means, we can plan our next move.'

'Perhaps we could solve the clue you have been given tonight.'

'Perhaps,' agreed Terry non-committally.

'You know,' pressed Mozz, 'I know these parts very well. I have travelled this region all my life. If you would share the clue with me, I may be able to help solve it.'

'That makes good sense,' replied Terry, 'but you have told me yourself that it is wise to be cautious. I would like to discuss that with my friends first. If they agree, we will tell you what the clue says. Perhaps you would give us some time together alone?'

'Very well,' said Mozz reluctantly. 'I will gather some firewood.'

As soon as Mozz was out of earshot, Terry called everyone together for an urgent conference. They huddled together on a grassy bank by the stream, so the noise of the gushing water would help drown out their voices.

'Keep a good look out for Mozz returning,' began Terry, looking warily in the direction Mozz had left. 'I am sorry that I have brought him into our company. I was wrong to trust him.'

'Don't blame yourself,' said Gwen, 'you had little choice anyway. The important thing is, what are we going to do? If we confront him at all, he will have the Bandero after us in no time. It is unlikely we could escape in time.'

'Polka says he has a plan,' said Terry, looking hopefully at Polka.

Polka nodded seriously. 'This is what we must do. Tonight, well after we have gone to bed, Terry and I will leave our tent. I will tread on a twig that I will have placed by Mozz's tent, but otherwise we will make no sound. We will head off down the stream together. Mozz will follow us. As soon as he has left, the rest of you must pack up only what is essential. Leave the tents, there will not be time to take them. Then you must lead all the morsk, including Mozz's, away from the camp.'

'Where do we take 'em?' asked Clumber, her eyes alight with excitement.

Polka surveyed the slopes of the small hill by which they had camped.

'Look, there is a small copse of trees on the northern side of the hill. You should wait on the far side.'

'What will you and Terry do?' asked Gwen uneasily.

'When we have led Mozz well away from the camp, we will split up, and double back. He can only follow one of us, and we will move quickly. So long as you are ready with our morsk saddled, we will reach you before him. Then we will ride off, taking his morsk, and he will be left behind.' The others considered this plan in silence for a while. Clumber was the first to pass judgement. 'Well, I reckon it's brilliant,' she said enthusiastically, patting Polka warmly on the back. Gwen was more measured in her response. 'It's risky,' she cautioned, 'you will have to return swiftly, because when you split up, he will realise some sort of trick is being played on him.'

'What if Mozz does not follow you and Terry?' asked Meeshka nervously.

'He will,' replied Polka emphatically, 'I know it.' A tense silence followed, in which everyone looked at Terry, for he had said nothing so far.

'Well,' he said guardedly, 'I think it is worth a try. We *have* to get rid of Mozz before we find the next stone, and I can't see how else we are going to do it. If he knew we had two stones already, he would probably call the Bandero down on us straight away. When he returns from collecting firewood, I will tell him that we will share the clue with him when we get back to Piree. He must give us time to take him completely into our trust.'

'If only we could solve the clue,' said Gwen anxiously. 'Then we would know where we must head next.'

'Oh,' said Polka casually, 'that was something else I meant to tell you. I have solved the clue.' Everyone looked at him in open-mouthed amazement.

'So what did the clue say?' asked Terry, glancing around warily for any sign of Mozz returning.

'It was simple,' explained Polka. 'You just rearrange the letters. NEW7 was NEW plus G, the seventh letter, and that makes GWEN. Then SNOW11 was SNOW plus K, which is KNOWS. And HERE23 was HERE plus W, which makes WHERE. So, *Gwen knows where* is the answer.' Everybody now turned to look in astonishment at Gwen.

'Oh, but I don't,' she said, shocked. 'There must be some mistake.'

'But you met Yalyf once,' said Terry.

'Yes, as a child. I was only about six.'

'But he spoke to you?'

'Well, yes, but I don't remember what he said.'

'Mozz returns,' warned Clumber. They turned to see Mozz coming back to the camp with a large bundle of firewood.

'OK, there's no time to work it out now,' said Terry briskly. 'We can worry about that later. Everyone try to be friendly to Mozz. He mustn't suspect that we are planning to abandon him tonight.'

Shadows in the Dark

Terry and Polka made no attempt to get any sleep before putting the plan into action. Through a crack in the tent opening, they watched a crescent moon turn from cream to orange, and slide lazily from view. Then, when they were sure it must have completely set, they ventured out of their tent and into the cool, dark night. Terry shivered as he stepped onto the damp grass, but whether this was the cold, or just nerves, he wasn't sure. Carefully, he knelt and re-tied the tent opening. Then he looked over at the dark form of the tent beside him. Inside, he knew that Gwen, Meeshka, and Clumber would be wide awake, listening intently for the sound of he and Polka leaving. He also knew that their hopes, and probably their freedom, rested on Polka and himself tonight. A tingle of anxiety ran through his body as he felt the weight of this responsibility.

The only sound on the night air was the constant babble of the stream, tumbling down the gentle slopes of the hill and cradling their campsite in a sweeping bend. Terry looked above him and found a sky that was full of fiercely shining stars. He saw that the constellation of Orion, the Hunter, had risen in the east, towering ominously over the Great Plain. Back home, the appearance of Orion was a sure sign that winter was setting in again. Whatever happened, he knew he would never look at it again without thinking of this night. Taking a deep breath, he nodded once to Polka, and they moved quietly over to where Mozz's tent was pitched, a short distance away. Within it, Terry now knew, was a dangerous Bandero spy, who would almost certainly be armed in some way. All of a sudden, the risks of Polka's plan seemed very real, but there could be no turning back now.

When Polka stepped deliberately on the twig he had placed close to Mozz's tent, it made a louder snap than either of them had anticipated. They both froze for a few moments, as if they genuinely didn't want to be heard, then without speaking, they set off into the night. Guided only by the sound of the stream, they soon intercepted its course and followed it eastwards.

'Do you think he's following?' whispered Terry when they were a reasonable distance from the campsite.

'I am certain he will be,' replied Polka softly, 'but we must not hang back or look behind us. He must not suspect we know he is there.'

'We need to give the others time to pack up. They won't dare come out of the tents until they are sure he is well away from the camp.'

'I know,' agreed Polka, 'but they will be keeping watch.

We should follow the stream until we find a good place to split up.'

As the land was predominantly flat, the course of the stream twisted and turned as it sought the lower ground, carving great S bends through the grassy plain. Once, as they traversed a particularly severe bend, Terry glanced over and felt certain he saw the familiar outline of Mozz, crouched down low by the water's edge. His pulse quickened, and he nudged Polka in the darkness to let him know they were definitely being followed.

They walked along the banks of the stream for several hundred metres, keeping a steady but unhurried pace, as if they knew exactly where they were heading. After several minutes, they came to a point where the northern bank was lined by alder trees. The silhouettes of the trees were inky black against the night sky, and their windswept branches leaned heavily out over the water. The stream itself widened considerably at this point, as the shallow water tumbled over a bed of large pebbles. It was the first point since the campsite that was easily fordable. Knowing that there may not be as good an opportunity again, both boys realised that the moment to split up had arrived.

'You hide one stone, and I will hide the other,' said Polka in a normal voice, making no attempt to whisper.

'OK,' replied Terry. 'You go that way, and I'll go the other. See you back at the tents.' Polka then crossed over the stream and headed off into the night. Terry paused only a moment, and then turned away from the stream and set off up the rising ground to his left, in the opposite direction to Polka. He walked briskly, but avoided the temptation to run. Now that he was on his own, he found that he had a heightened sense of awareness. The swish of his feet through the coarse grass, no longer masked by the stream's babble, seemed suddenly loud. He wished he had had the opportunity to practise the route he needed to take in the daylight, because at night time, it was doubly difficult to be sure of your position. He did not want to get too far from the stream, for fear of losing his way, but nor did he want to walk straight back into his pursuer. The ground rose slightly in the direction he was heading, and when he crested this rise, he deemed it time to turn back towards the campsite. Stealing a quick glance behind him, his suspicions were confirmed – he saw a shadow traverse the top of the risen ground. It was cleverly and quickly done, by someone obviously practised in the art of covert trailing, but Terry was left in no doubt. He had expected that Mozz would choose to follow him, rather than Polka. Now it was down to him alone to try and lose the Bandero officer. Fighting back feelings of panic, he decided to quicken his pace, and broke into a steady trot. By now, Mozz must have realised he was not going to hide a stone after all. Maybe that meant that Mozz could jump him at any moment?

The further Terry travelled over the featureless ground, the more anxious he became about finding his way to the copse of trees. The starlight was little help for getting his bearings. The deep darkness of night time in Gwen's world, that previously he had marvelled at, was now a troubling hindrance. He could vaguely hear the tinkle of water away to his left, and he realised that because he was taking a more direct route back, avoiding the bends of the stream, it would not take as long to reach the campsite. He decided to alter his course slightly to the right. His hope was to convince Mozz that he had simply missed the campsite in the confusion of the dark.

All the time, he urgently scanned the horizon for anything that might be the copse of trees, but he saw nothing. The dark shadow of the hill was unmistakeable at least, and it seemed further away than it ought to be. Thinking that perhaps he had altered course too far to the right, and missed the copse altogether, he turned left and moved back towards the hill. Then he heard a sound behind him, as if somebody had slipped on the damp grass. There was a dull thud, and it sounded alarmingly close. If it was Mozz, he was *too* close, so Terry broke into a run. By now he had little idea of which direction he should head in. It was proving so much harder to find his way than he had expected, and new surges of panic started to wash over him. This time, they were not so easy to quell. In the daylight, the route had seemed straight forward, but now it was as if the copse of trees had never existed – he could see no sign of it. Then he tripped and fell himself, adding to his disorientation. The land ahead of him was definitely rising, so he knew he must be on the hillside again. Fighting his impulse to keep running, he stopped to listen. To his great relief, he clearly heard the stream ahead of him, and this helped give him some idea of where he was. He turned once again, this time to his right, and ran in a sweeping curve back down to where he felt the copse of trees should be. Then he stopped dead in his tracks – a shadowy figure stood ahead of him. At first he was sure it was Mozz, and with a sinking heart he knew it was over – he had been caught. He tried a futile dodge to the left, expecting the dark shape to make a leap for him, but it made no move. Terry was nonplussed by this, and as he stood still himself, he began to realise that the dark shadow was too small to be Mozz – it was smaller even than himself.

'Polka?' he whispered in confusion. The effect on the shadow was considerable. It twisted towards him at lightning speed, and hissed with surprise, like a startled cat.

For a second, a green light seemed to glow in its eyes, and it hissed again.

'*Stones!*'

Terry was absolutely petrified. Not in the way he was frightened of Mozz, or the other Bandero. This was a new kind of fear he had never experienced before, and he didn't know how to deal with it. Like in a bad dream, he was completely unable to move his arms and legs. Unlike a dream though, he knew that this was real. He wasn't about to wake up somewhere safe. All he could do was stare helplessly as the creature started to edge slowly towards him. Then Terry noticed a change. Whatever the creature was, it was beginning to fade away into the darkness. As it advanced, it reached out towards him with long arms, but before it could get hold of him, it simply dissolved into the night.

As relief flooded into him, Terry had the strange sensation of wanting to burst into tears. He had no idea what he had just seen, but it was the most frightening moment of his life. He stood a moment longer, until the shock began to wear off. Then he no longer cared which direction he was heading in – he simply wanted to get away from the terrifying shadow. Running with reckless abandon, he raced down the hillside. He did not see the copse of trees until he was actually running through it. The tangled undergrowth within it tripped him once more, sending him sprawling amongst a patch of gorse. He heard, rather than saw something enter the copse behind him. Frantically, he struggled to his feet and pressed on, but it was almost impossible to make progress, with unseen vegetation constantly snagging him. Through the silhouette of trees ahead of him, he could see what looked like a group of morsk, standing in a dark huddle beyond the copse. He struck out towards them, but couldn't penetrate the thick bushes that stood between him and the open terrain. He floundered around, falling as he tried to force a way through, and making a great deal of noise. Each time he clambered to his feet, he could feel the energy being sapped from his legs. And all the time, from behind him, the heavy sounds of his pursuit were getting closer.

'Run,' he cried weakly to his friends. 'Go without me.'

Then suddenly, against all expectation, he seemed to break free of the bushes. The last snag on his clothing snapped free, and hope flooded back into him. He had a chance, just a chance, to make it. Bursting out of the copse, he made a last desperate lunge towards his friends. 'Run,' he cried again, but even as he did so, two strong arms enclosed him, and wrestled him heavily to the ground. Someone landed on top of him, pinning him helplessly so that he could not move.

'Enough of this, youngster!' said an angry voice in his left ear. 'Whatever your trick, it has failed. You are going nowhere tonight.'

Khyme

There was a long pause, in which nothing seemed to happen. Mozz did not relax his grip, but nor did he say anything more. Terry remained pinned face down on the ground, just at the edge of the copse of trees. Then a man's voice, which wasn't Mozz's, spoke clearly and calmly in the darkness.

'You can feel the knife to your back, towman. If you move, it will be the last thing you feel.' Terry said nothing, mostly because he had no idea what was happening. Then the man spoke again, more loudly. 'Gwen, if you are over there, would you quickly bring some rope.'

'Hev?' came Gwen's faltering reply from some distance away, 'is that you?'

'Yes, Gwen, but please make haste with the rope.' Terry heard some frantic rummaging in a saddlebag, and the sound of footsteps running over towards them.

'Bind his hands, and his legs,' said Hev, 'as tightly as you can.' When Gwen had done this, Hev checked the knots carefully. Only when he was satisfied that Mozz was securely bound did he roll him over onto his back, allowing Terry to scramble to his feet.

'Perhaps someone can explain what has been happening,' Hev said, embracing Gwen tenderly.

'The towman, Mozz, is a Bandero spy,' replied Gwen through tears of joy at seeing her husband safe and well. 'We were trying to escape from him in the dark, but he caught Terry before we could get away.'

'That part I know,' answered Hev. 'I was camped for the night in this copse.'

Meeshka and Polka shyly appeared out of the darkness to greet Hev, having left Clumber holding the halters of all six morsk.

'So, the group is complete,' continued Hev as he greeted Meeshka and Polka.

'And one more besides,' replied Gwen happily, 'looking after the morsk.'

'But how do you come to be here?' he asked perplexed, 'so far east on the plain.'

'For now, a full explanation must wait,' said Gwen firmly, 'because the Bandero are on our trail, and we do not have long. Also, I do not wish to speak in front of the spy. What should we do with him?' Hev looked down with distaste at the man lying trussed at his feet. 'I propose that if the Bandero are truly on your trail, we leave him to be found by them. A few hours discomfort will be fair recompense for my days in the castle dungeons.'

'You will not get far,' growled Mozz angrily, 'and when you are caught, there will be a high price to pay for you all.

If you have any sense, you will release me now and put yourself at the Baron's mercy.'

'I think not,' replied Hev cheerfully. 'Having met the Baron personally, I suspect that it is you who will shortly be at his mercy.' Leaving Mozz to reflect on that sober fact, they returned to the morsk and Hev was introduced to Clumber. Then they discussed in hushed tones what they should do next.

'My morsk is tethered on the other side of the copse,' said Hev. 'Let's go there first, and we can talk out of earshot of the Bandero spy.' As they made their way around the trees, Gwen gave Hev a hurried account of how Clumber had joined them at Piree, and of their journey north to meet the Watcher in the Ravine of Silence. Hev listened with interest as she explained that they now had two stones, but although they had solved the next clue, she had not been able to understand it.

'Well,' said Hev grimly as he retrieved his morsk, 'we have a day – two at the most. Then every Bandero in the Realm will be looking for us, and I've no doubt the Baron will make it worth their while to find us. We need to disappear completely.'

'But we must find the other stones,' replied Gwen desperately. 'Perhaps we should return to Herstan and Freda's to hide for a while.'

'I fear that will be putting our good friends at risk if we do, but it may be our only option.'

Terry nodded hopefully. 'I don't know what we would have done without all the help people have given us,' he said gratefully.

'It was meant to be,' smiled Gwen.

'That may be truer than you think,' added Hev. 'When

I was imprisoned in the Castle, the Baron showed me a letter. It was not signed, nor was it addressed, but I suspect it was written by Yalyf, and intended for you Gwen.'

'For me? What did it say?'

'That he met you as a child, and said something to you. That a boy would be coming, and that it would be your destiny to help him. And something about the castle becoming what it was built for.'

'Hellaine told me about that letter!' cried Terry eagerly. 'She said that Yalyf had murmured in his sleep that they could find the letter!'

'So,' replied Hev thoughtfully, 'it all ties up. Yalyf has left this letter in the castle. He must have hoped that somehow he would be able to get it to you, Gwen.'

'To help you remember!' said Meeshka.

'What's this?' asked Hev.

Gwen sighed. 'I mentioned that we did not understand the next clue. It suggests that I would be able to say where the next stone is.'

Hev looked at her in surprise. 'How could that be so?'

'I don't know,' she replied miserably.

'Wait a sec,' said Terry suddenly. 'The clue said *Gwen knows where*.'

'Yes, but I *don't*.'

'OK,' continued Terry, 'but Yalyf must have *thought* that you would.'

Gwen simply shrugged in bewilderment.

'Now this letter said that he told you something once,' Terry persisted excitedly, 'and didn't you say that you only met Yalyf once? That he spoke to you, but you didn't understand what he said?'

'Yes, that's true?'

'And that this happened by a well?'

'Yes.'

'Could he have said something about the well?'

Gwen froze like a statue, as she considered Terry's question. Nobody spoke. Gwen was staring at Terry, but her mind was looking back twenty years into the past. And as she looked, the muscles on her anxious face began to relax.

'I think he might have,' she said slowly. 'It is difficult to be certain, but a strange phrase has just come into my mind. I think..., I do think I remember something. I could be mistaken, but perhaps it was something like *the water will not harm it*. I know that it made no sense to me at the time.'

'But now it makes perfect sense!' cried Terry, 'the stone is down the well!'

This announcement caused considerable excitement amongst them all, with everybody trying to talk at once.

'It has to be!'

'It would be a good hiding place.'

'Are you sure, Gwen?'

'It can only be down the well!'

'Where is the well?'

'Quiet!' said Hev sternly at last, 'or our unwelcome guest will hear you, even from the other side of this copse.'

'Oh, but I do think Terry is right,' whispered Gwen happily. 'The well is in the village I grew up in. It is called Khyme, and it is only two hours ride, *east* of Piree.'

Terry considered this carefully. 'Mozz thought we were about a day's ride east of Piree at the moment. Does that mean we could reach this village tonight?'

'No, we would have to rest the morsk at some point,' replied Hev after some consideration.

'And rest ourselves, too,' added Gwen. 'Also, unless we

go back for them, we will not have the tents.'

'I'd prefer to put some distance between us and the Bandero,' murmured Terry cautiously, 'and there is something else.'

'What is it, Terry?' asked Gwen with concern.

'Back there on the hill, when I was running from Mozz. I saw a dark shadowy figure. It wasn't Mozz.'

'Are you sure?'

'Positive. It was smaller than me, and as it came towards me, it sort of hissed the word *stones*. Then it just seemed to dissolve. It was the scariest thing I've ever seen in my life.'

There was an ominous silence, broken finally by Clumber. 'Sans-Schen,' she said gravely.

'Well..., I can't say for sure, but maybe.'

'What is this you speak of?' asked Hev seriously. Gwen explained briefly what little Hellaine had been able to tell them about the mysterious threat. Meeshka glanced around warily as she spoke, imagining shadows in the darkness.

'As if the Bandero are not enough to worry about' said Hev ruefully when Gwen had finished. 'I have never heard of these Sans-Schen, but they are all the more reason for us to make haste now. I suggest we press on immediately, and stop at dawn. We can use the daylight to find a sheltered spot with a good view of the plain. We will post a watch and make sure we are not taken by surprise. Then when both we and the morsk are rested sufficiently, we can press on to Khyme. With luck, we should be there by nightfall.'

'That sounds good to me,' agreed Terry enthusiastically. 'When we have the next stone, perhaps we could then make for Piree. When we get there we can decide what to do about the Bandero.'

'Then it's agreed,' said Hev, climbing into his saddle.

'Cast the towman's morsk free. It will likely follow us anyway, but we can't afford to be slowed by it. Empty the saddlebags of anything unnecessary – we must ride like the wind.'

Although the moon was long set, they were crossing the true Plain of Carthag now, and the terrain was perfectly flat for mile after mile. Although they could not always risk the gallop, they never moved at less than a good canter, and suffered no mishap. An hour before dawn, their trail merged with a well worn path, heading due west. Here at last, was a proper road on which to ride, and they pressed the morsk into a sustained gallop.

Just as the first shaft of direct sunlight broke free from the horizon behind them, they stopped to find a place to rest. The blood red light bathed the plain ahead in a deep, warm glow, strangely at odds with the penetrating chill of the frosty morning air. Hev had chosen a point where the road passed over a wide stream. They turned north from here and rode for a mile up its shallow bed. Leaving the morsk under the shade of a group of willow trees, where the grazing was good, they climbed on foot over raised ground to their east. They soon reached a small rounded summit, covered in tall, yellow gorse bushes. Looking south, there was a clear view all the way back to the bridge. To the east, the road was visible for many miles.

'If we are pursued,' said Hev, 'we will see the Bandero well before they reach the bridge. Then, if they spot that our trail has left the road, they will have to guess correctly whether we rode north or south along the stream. This is as safe as we can make ourselves.'

'We may as well eat what food we have left,' said Gwen. 'Later tonight, I hope we will be safely in Piree.'

Although cool, it was a bright sunny day, and in amongst the shelter of the gorse, they were able to make themselves very comfortable. After their breakfast, they agreed a watch rota, and then huddled down amongst the bushes. There was not a breath of wind, and the sunlight kept them pleasantly warm as they slept. The sun climbed up through a cloudless sky, and down on the plain, nothing stirred. They were able to get several hours of much needed rest.

Back on the road again, they felt refreshed and ready for any challenge. The morsk too, clearly had more vigour about their stride. To everyone's great relief, there was still no sign of pursuit. Terry began to feel confident that they would not be caught. 'Even if the Bandero picked up our trail through the lakes,' he yelled as they rode, 'they should only just be finding Mozz about now.'

'Let's hope you're right,' answered Hev, more soberly.

They stopped once more, only briefly, to rest and water the morsk. They were back in territory that Gwen recognised, and were only about an hour from Khyme. At Gwen's suggestion, when they resumed their journey, she went ahead with Meeshka and Polka, while Terry, Hev and Clumber lagged five minutes behind. They were now meeting the occasional travellers on the road, and they did not want to be seen all together. If the Bandero were following them, they would be asking about a group of two adults and four children, so it seemed a good idea to split up. Those travellers they met, they simply bade 'gooday' to, and avoided being drawn into conversation.

During the late afternoon a few clouds had appeared in the west, and as these turned orange with the setting sun, the white stone houses of Khyme appeared in the distance.

Tired but relieved, Gwen, Meeshka and Polka waited on the outskirts of the village for the others to catch up. Then they moved off the road and into the fields, remaining hidden until darkness had fully enveloped the small village.

When Gwen had been a child, Khyme was just a small village of no more than twenty houses, clustered either side of the road. Now though, there were many more properties, and dark cobbled streets led north and south from the main road. Most of the houses were shuttered up for the night, and they heard only occasional sounds from within. The streets themselves were empty.

'These days,' said Gwen quietly, 'the village takes its water from an underground aqueduct, linked to the north canal. Most of the new houses have been built close to this. The old well is at the western end – I just hope it has not been blocked up.' She led them to a grassy area at the far end of the village and they spread out to search. They soon found a small stone circle, protruding up out of the knee-length grass. The wooden hood and drawing mechanism had been removed, but the opening was still clear, and Gwen was in no doubt that it was the old village well. They looked down into its dark and murky depths with some trepidation.

'I wonder how deep it is,' said Meeshka anxiously.

'Only one way to find out,' said Terry, 'let's get the rope and lower me down.'

There was an unspoken understanding that Terry would be the one to go down the well, and not even Gwen objected when Hev began to tie a harness around Terry's waist. Hev also retrieved and lit a small torch from his own saddlebag.

'Take this' he said, 'you will need light at the bottom of

the well. Take care, for it won't be easy, trying to manage the rope and hold on to the torch.'

'I'll be OK,' replied Terry, eager to make the descent.

Although there was no-one around, Gwen was nervous that they might be surprised.

Clumber reluctantly agreed to keep watch a short distance from the well, on the eastern side of the village, just in case the Bandero should arrive.

'Alright then, but you gotta tell me everythin' what happens,' she said grumpily.

When Hev was certain the rope was secure, Terry climbed over the lip, holding the rope in one hand and the torch in the other.

'Watch you don't burn your rope with the torch,' advised Gwen. 'We would never get you out again without help.'

'Good luck, and be careful,' added Meeshka nervously.

Hev had wrapped the rope around his body, and propping his feet against the well wall, he took Terry's weight and slowly began to lower him into the well.

Terry had done some abseiling before, and after his experience in the ravine, this felt easy. He balanced with his feet against the inner wall of the well, and pushed off to drop a few feet each time.

'What can you see?' asked Polka impatiently.

'The stone is damp and slippery,' replied Terry, his voice echoing strangely. 'I've nearly reached the water.'

He managed to judge his last drop so his feet came to rest just above the water level. He paused and adjusted his grip on the rope, allowing himself the freedom to hold the torch away from his body. He twisted around to look behind and then below. The water still looked black as tar under the torchlight.

'I'm going to try and stand in the water,' he shouted up.

'OK,' replied Hev, loosening the strain on the rope slightly.

Terry pushed off from the wall and straightened his body, dropping several feet all at once and ending up to his waist in the cold water. Finding no purchase for his feet, his weight kept him pressed tight up against the side of the well, with his fingers trapped between the rope and the stone. Crucially though, he had managed to hang on to the torch with his other hand.

'The water's freezing!' he gasped, 'and it's too deep to stand up.'

'Are you OK?' asked Gwen, leaning dangerously over the side.

Terry did not answer until he had managed to get his feet propped against the side of the well again. His legs were still in the water, and his purchase was slippery.

'Yeah, I'm OK, but the water's deep, and I can't see down into it with the torch. If the stone's at the bottom, I'm never going to find it like this. I think we're going to have to wait until daylight!'

'Alright!' replied Gwen. 'Hev will pull you back up.' After the long ride, and the anticipation of finding the third stone, everyone was disappointed. But there seemed to be no other option – they would have to give up for tonight. It would mean going into Piree, and returning at dawn.

'The trouble is,' said Hev to Gwen quietly, 'if we wait until daylight we may well have the Bandero for company.'

'I know,' she answered grimly, helping Hev haul on the rope to bring Terry up.

As they tugged together, Terry suddenly shouted from down below.

'Wait! Hang on a minute!'

He was about five feet above the water level, and a particular stone in the side of the well wall had caught his eye. It had a large letter T carved deeply into its face. In his eagerness to get down to the water, he had missed it on his descent.

'What is it,' shouted Polka from above, 'have you found something?'

'Is it the tumblestone?' asked Meeshka excitedly.

Terry was exploring the block of stone with his fingers, and found that it was loose.

'Just wait a minute,' he shouted back.

He managed to get his fingers into the small crevice around the stone, and by rocking it to and fro he was able to work it gradually out of the wall. It took a while, but eventually the stone came completely loose and fell with a mighty splash into the water below.

'What's happening?' shouted Gwen from above.

'One of the stones was loose. It had a letter T on it,' he yelled. 'I'm going to see if I can reach into the hole.'

He twisted and turned, hanging on the rope, and trying to find a comfortable position from which to leave go and get his arm into the cavity. The trouble was that he still needed to keep hold of the torch with his other arm. He was soaked from the waist down, both his arms were aching, and he was starting to shiver with the cold, but at last he was able to manoeuvre into a position from which he could reach inside. The first thing he felt was sand, and his fingers dug into it and explored. Below him, he could hear the water in the well sloshing around in an odd way, but he could spare no attention to consider it at that moment.

'Terry?' It was Meeshka's voice. 'What's that light?'

Terry had his cheek right up against the cold wet wall of the well, as he reached as far as possible into the hole. 'Hang on a sec!' he said breathlessly. His fingers, had felt something, just out of reach. Working delicately with his finger tips, stretching as far as he could, he managed to bring the object slowly towards him.

'Terry! There's a light in the water!'

'The water's swirling around!'

'What's happening down there?'

Terry was aware that his friends at the top of the well felt something was not right. He knew they were trying to warn him about something, but all of his attention was consumed in bringing the object he had felt out of the cavity. He could hear lots of people shouting down to him at once, but he was interested only in the small wooden box he had managed to extract from the hole. He was able to jam the torch against the wall with one of his feet, freeing both hands to examine the box more closely. It was only the size of his hand, and had a tight fitting lid with no catch. He pondered whether to wait until he was out of the well before opening it, but curiosity got the better of him, and he pulled off the lid and looked inside. The torch slipped from beneath his foot as he did so, and fell with a loud hiss into the water below. Never mind, he thought, it didn't matter now. It did not occur to Terry that he still had plenty of light to examine the contents of the box, even though he had dropped his torch. He continued to ignore the excitement at the top of the well.

In the box, he found something had been wrapped in paper. Carefully, he unfolded the paper, which he noticed had writing on, and into his palm fell a beautiful smooth stone. It was a silvery grey, and shone like a star in the yellow light from beneath his feet.

'I've found it!' he shouted triumphantly, 'I've found the next stone!' He glanced at the paper and read the writing:

This is Haematite. The next clue is:

AG

UA

OT SUAZN UL LUATZGOT

Another clue to be solved. He put the paper safely in his pocket, but kept hold of the stone. Feeling very satisfied, he called up to his friends above. 'It's OK, you can pull me up now!'

It was only then that Terry realised all was not as it should have been. He could hear everyone still shouting above him, but in such a confused and frantic manner that he wasn't able to make any sense of what they were saying. Then he looked down, and found that a golden glow was emanating from underneath the water. Not only that, the water's surface was swirling around like a whirlpool. There was something horribly familiar about it. Then as he watched, a golden torus broke up through the surface of the water, splattering water noisily against the sides of the well. It was already spinning at incredible speed and emitting a low pitched hum. At the same instant, he felt a sudden change in the air around him – a sort of treacly stickiness. Then too many things started happening at once. He heard Clumber's voice, riding over the top of the other commotion in its shrill urgency.

'Some riders are coming! I reckon it's maybe Bandero!'

Then there was a muddle of other excited voices:

'Polka! It is! It's the torus! Quickly!'

'Meeshka! No! Hev, don't let her!'

'I can't hold the rope!'

Terry felt the rope give, and he started to fall back, but he was not alone – Meeshka and Polka had leapt down into the well with him. They did not fall as far as the water though – somehow the air supported them. All three of them were swirling around in the vortex formed by the torus, but in the confined space of the well, it all seemed a jumble of different arms and legs. Terry finally realised what was happening. At first, his heart leapt with hope – was he on his way home at last? But his hopes sank as he remembered the voice in the Huntsman's Cottage. *You cannot return until you have the seven tumblestones*, it had said.

The rope had broken, and hung loosely around his waist. He could only wait for the inevitable. In the final moments, he looked up and was aware of two things. First, was the beauty and grace of Gwen's headlong dive into the turmoil – whatever was happening, Gwen had decided she would be a part of it. Second was Clumber's face at the top of the well, stunningly lit from below by the golden light. Her mouth was wide open in pure astonishment. Then Terry closed his eyes, as the vortex took them. He had no idea what was going to happen, but his hand was still clasped tightly around the third stone.

Did you know?

You can buy the three tumblestones that Terry and his friends have found, together with the black bag, from **Crystal Fantasy**.

Just visit
www.crystalfantasy.co.uk

Crystal Fantasy
are the only authorised supplier of tumblestones for
Terry, the Torus and the Tumblestones.

If you have enjoyed *The Seven Stones*, why not reserve your copy of the second book in this series?

The Pale Death Moon
C. P. Goy

Just visit
www.terry-torus-tumblestones.co.uk

A copy of *The Pale Death Moon* will be reserved in your name, and you will be notified when it is available for purchase. You will also receive information about the publication of the final book in this series:

The Guardian of the Past
C. P. Goy.

Coming soon…

Book Two
The Pale Death Moon
C. P. Goy

The Torus has saved Terry, Gwen, Meeshka and Polka from the Bandero, but deposited them in a completely new world, where idyllic sandy beaches give way to untamed tropical forests. They soon learn from new friends, Pendu and Tayba, that Yalyf has been there before them - three more riddles must be solved, three more stones must be found. But it's not going to be straightforward. The evil Ackru has already stolen one of the stones, and now he is making sacrifices each full moon, to appease the 'Black Spirits' who have started to appear on the island. When Pendu is captured, it becomes a desperate race against time. Polka will need his best plan ever, because the next full moon is only three nights away…

Book Three
The Guardian of the Past
C. P. Goy

Back in Gwen's world, and re-united with Hev and Clumber, the friends realise that the key to the mystery lies somewhere in the infamous Castle Turuk – but breaking into the Baron's fortress is considered impossible – by everyone, that is, except Polka. All the perplexing strands of the puzzle start to come together, as Terry begins to understand the incredible truth. The stunning secret, hidden from them all for so long, is finally revealed, and Terry's greatest test is now before him. If he is to save all three worlds, and set the future back on the right track, he must find within himself the greatest trust of all – to trust himself.